Third Factory

Viktor Shklovsky
THIRD FACTORY

Introduction and Translation
by Richard Sheldon

Afterword by Lyn Hejinian

Dalkey Archive Press

Shklovskii, Viktor Borisovich, 1893-1984
    [Tret'ia fabrika. English]
    Third factory / Viktor Shklovsky; translated with an introduction by
    Richard Sheldon; afterword by Lyn Hejinian.
        p. cm.
    Previously published: Ann Arbor : Ardis, 1977.
    ISBN 1-56478-317-0 (pbk.: alk. paper)
        I. Sheldon, Richard (Richard Robert) II. Hejinian, Lyn. III. Title.
    PG3476.S488 T713 2002
    891.73'42--dc21
                                                                      2002073505

Partially funded by a grant from the Illinois Arts Council, a state agency.

Dalkey Archive Press books are published by the Center for Book Culture, a
nonprofit organization with offices in Chicago and Normal, Illinois.

www.centerforbookculture.org

Printed on permanent/durable acid-free paper and bound in the United
States of America.

CONTENTS

INTRODUCTION: VIKTOR SHKLOVSKY AND THE
DEVICE OF OSTENSIBLE SURRENDER

One frequently discussed problem in Western approaches to post-revolutionary Russian literature has been the temptation to identify "rebels against" and to praise their work out of proportion to its merits. One notable exception to this pattern is Viktor Shklovsky, one of the earliest and most outspoken defenders of creative freedom in the Soviet Union. Though his books and articles were viciously attacked by the Marxist critics throughout the twenties, Western critics, viewing those same books and articles from the distance imposed by time and place, have viewed them as a series of surrenders that hastened or even precipitated the collapse of the Formalist movement.

The first of these surrenders is thought to be *Zoo, or Letters Not about Love*, 1923;[1] the second is this book, *Third Factory*, 1926;[2] the third is "A Monument to Scientific Error," 1930.[3] After this third and most abject surrender, according to the prevailing view, Shklovsky toed the line, submitting to Party pressure for the privilege of publishing works markedly inferior to his early books. This view is not supported by the facts.

Shklovsky's role as a defender of creative freedom began immediately after the February revolution, when a struggle developed between the Commission on Art Affairs and the Union of Artists.[4] Gorky had organized the Commission to take charge of preserving the monuments and artifacts of the past from excesses of revolutionary zeal, but it was given, in addition, the power to regulate the construction of new monuments. The Union, organized on March 5, the day after the formation of Gorky's Commission, was composed of people like Zdanevich, Sologub, Brik, Mayakovsky and Shklovsky, who feared that Gorky's conservatism might prejudice the cause of avant-garde art. In April, this group appointed a delegation to meet with the Soviet of Ministers and the Soviet of Workers' and Soldiers' Councils, which were persuaded to curtail the power of Gorky's Commission. Throughout March, April and May, Shklovsky made a series of speeches accusing Gorky of prejudice against the Futurists and of seeking to impose his ideas on the avant-garde.

In May, the Provisional Government appointed Shklovsky

commissar attached to the Russian army. He served in this capacity during the ill-fated Kerensky offensive that summer and, at his request, was transferred to the Russian army of occupation in Persia in September. When he returned to Petrograd in January, 1918, after the withdrawal of the army from Persia, he joined the Union for the Rebirth of Russia, an underground organization plotting to restore the Constituent Assembly. When that group was broken up, he fled to the Ukraine in the fall of 1918. Only in January, 1919, with help from Gorky, was he pardoned for these activities and allowed to return to Petrograd.[5]

During his absence, the conflict between Gorky's Commission and the Union had been decided in a manner that spelled defeat for both sides. After the October revolution, Anatoly Lunacharsky, the new Commissar of Education, persuaded some members of the Union—including Tatlin, Khlebnikov, Brik and Mayakovsky—to resign and join the Governing Board of the newly created State Soviet for Art Affairs. This is one of the ways in which the new regime expressed its displeasure with Gorky, who had not endeared himself to Lenin with his powerful campaign against the Bolsheviks during the months preceding the October revolution.[6] The Futurists thus achieved the power that enabled them to celebrate the first anniversary of the revolution by decorating the streets and squares of Petrograd with geometric designs. The Union, objecting strongly to cooperation with the government, protested the defection of some of its leading members. At a protest meeting held on April 7, 1918, the Union joined forces with the infuriated Gorky, who was elected their presiding officer, but nothing could be done. By the end of the year, the Union had dissolved.

In December, 1918, under the aegis of Lunacharsky's *Narkompros*, there appeared a weekly newspaper called *Art of the Commune (Iskusstvo kommuny)*, published by Osip Brik. This newspaper became the stronghold for the so-called left-wing Futurists and the literary organ through which Mayakovsky disseminated his views. In particular, he and Brik, anticipating the platform of LEF, proclaimed the poet's obligation to his society and the need to discard not only the art of the past, but perhaps all art[7]—a position to which Shklovsky objects in his comments on Brik in this book.

Shklovsky, then, returned from eighteen months of battle on various fronts to find the Union, of which he had been a leader, defunct. Worse yet, his Futurist comrades, who had argued before the revolution that the artist has no civic responsibility, were now comfortably ensconced in positions of power under the new Bolshevik government and were imposing their artistic predilections upon their fellow artists—a practice which the Union had furiously protested when Gorky had tried it. Shklovsky bitterly opposed the dangerous notion propounded by Mayakovsky and Brik that art must reflect the new class ideology. In this connection, he made his famous statement: "Art has always been free of life; its flag has never reflected the color of the flag flying over the city fortress."[8] This statement, which sounds as though it were aimed at the Bolsheviks, was actually addressed to those Futurists like Mayakovsky and Brik who had meekly accepted positions in the civil service of the new regime. Shklovsky saw in this act the end of Futurism, "one of the highest attainments of man's genius," and he added, all too prophetically: "The mistakes now being made are so clear to me and will be so painful to art that it is impossible to keep quiet about them. . . . Comrades, this is certainly the surrender of all positions! This is Belinsky-Vengerov and *The History of the Russian Intelligentsia*. . . . That rustling tail of newspaper editorials being prepared for it [art] offends the eye."[9]

This is strong language. Shklovsky's book *Knight's Move (Khod konia)* contains many such complaints and admonitions. At the beginning of the book, he tells about the millipede that functioned marvelously well until the day that a turtle asked how it managed to coordinate the motion of all those legs. Then the millipede began thinking about where each leg was:

> It introduced centralization, chancellorization, bureaucratism and could no longer budge even one leg.
> Then it said, "Viktor Shklovsky was right when he said, 'The greatest misfortune of our time is that we regulate art without knowing what it is. The greatest misfortune of Russian

art is that we scorn it like a husk of rice. And yet art is anything but a vehicle for propaganda, just as vitalin, which food must contain in addition to proteins and fats, is neither protein nor fat, and yet the life of the organism is impossible without it.' "

The greatest misfortune of Russian art is that it is not allowed to move organically the way the heart moves in a man's chest: it is being regulated like the movement of trains.

"Citizens and comrades," said the millipede, "look at me and you will see the folly of over-regulation! Comrades in revolution, comrades in war, leave art at liberty, not in its own name, but in the name of the fact that it is impossible to regulate the unknown!"[10]

From 1919 through 1921, Shklovsky worked feverishly with Zamyatin to propagate the idea of art as pure form, as having no obligations to the real world. He developed his ideas at the meetings of *Opoyaz* and the Serapion Brothers, whose members were enormously influenced. Then in the spring of 1922, the charges based on his anti-Bolshevik activity of 1918 were revived and he fled to Finland to escape arrest. In the summer of 1922, he joined the Russian colony in Berlin, where he published the first of his trilogy of surrenders, *Zoo, or Letters Not about Love.*

Zoo, or Letters Not about Love, has been described by Professor Erlich as a book in which "Shklovsky had symbolically 'surrendered' to the powers that be."[11] The main evidence for this position is the last letter in the book, a petition to the Central Committee wherein Shklovsky, lamenting his loss of youth and self-assurance, specifically raises his hands in surrender. Another Western critic, speaking of the elegy to Khlebnikov in the fourth letter, mentions that Shklovsky was the first to compare Khlebnikov's fate to that of Christ and says that Shklovsky, "considering it inevitable that the state should neglect and reject the heretical visionary, absolved it of blame for his death, writing that even those who crucified Christ were 'no more guilty than the nails.' "[12]

Both of these opinions overlook the context in which Shklovsky's remarks are made. It is true that the first half of the concluding letter is an appeal for amnesty, but the subservience of the appeal is countered by the last half of the letter, where Shklovsky tells that the Turkish soldiers who surrendered to the Russians at the battle of Erzerum were massacred on the spot. He insinuates that this may very well be the fate that he can expect from the Bolsheviks if he returns. It is interesting that the censors removed this portion of the letter from the 1964 edition of *Zoo, or Letters Not about Love,* leaving the surrender to stand alone, without the anecdote that contradicts it.

As for the notion that the elegy is a piece that absolves the state of blame for the death of Khlebnikov, nothing could be further from the truth. Antony did not really believe that Brutus was an honorable man, nor does Shklovsky believe that the state is guiltless in the death of Khlebnikov. Professor Piper has failed to recognize the bitter irony of that passage. Once again, it is interesting to note that the very passage where Shklovsky comments that the state is not responsible for the death of human beings has been cut by the censors from the 1964 edition. Its ironic import was evident to them.

What has been overlooked in these interpretations, and elsewhere, is simply the fact that the hallmark of Shklovsky's style is contradiction. He explains in *Hamburg Account* that he assembled his books in such a way that adjacent pieces are in a contradictory relationship.[13] One can find a plethora of surrenders in his books if one removes seemingly conciliatory statements from their context, where they are usually contradicted. In *A Sentimental Journey,* for example, one finds the following sequence, which is a useful paradigm of his method: "But if we had been asked then, 'Who are you for—Kaledin, Kornilov or the Bolsheviks?,' Task and I would have chosen the Bolsheviks."[14] That statement sounds quite conciliatory. In the following sentence, though, Shklovsky says, "However, in a certain comedy, the harlequin was asked, 'Do you prefer to be hanged or quartered?' He answered, 'I prefer soup.' "

Contradiction is found throughout *A Sentimental Journey* and is even more deeply embedded in *Zoo, or Letters Not about Love.* The counterpoint of obedience and defiance found in the surrender letter runs throughout the book, which is only ostensibly not about love. In fact, every perfunctory attempt to discuss another subject fails and is repudiated by the reappearance of the forbidden theme.

What about *Third Factory*, the second of Shklovsky's ostensible surrenders? Professor Erlich mentions only the conciliatory statements without referring to the defiant statements that serve as retractions, and he speaks of the "malaise" that pervades *Third Factory*.[15] Professor Piper describes this book as an extraordinary volte-face and speaks of how Shklovsky, despite "the lack of freedom in the Soviet Union," decided to remain and to surrender himself to the times. "*Tret'ia fabrika*," says Professor Piper unequivocally, "destroyed formalism."[16]

"Malaise" refers to a spiritual crisis whose cause is vague or unknown. Shklovsky had his reasons for what might more accurately be described as anguish. As a right-wing SR, he had fought on two fronts in the service of the Provisional Government. After the overthrow of that government by the Bolsheviks, he had joined an underground movement to overthrow the Bolsheviks. Forced into emigration by these activities, he had lived for more than a year in Berlin and had discovered that he was organically incapable of living abroad. He had returned home in the fall of 1923 and, despite his "bad record" and shaky position, had resumed his connections with the much-maligned Serapion Brothers[17] and had joined LEF, the coalition of Futurists and members of *Opoyaz* founded by Mayakovsky in 1923. Shklovsky quickly became one of the most important members of LEF. Its collapse early in 1925 contributed to the anguish that underlies *Third Factory*.

The central cause of his anguish, however, was clearly the resolution of the Central Committee, "On Party Policy in the Field of Imaginative Literature," promulgated on June 18, 1925.[18] This resolution grew out of the attempts of the proletarian writers, through their organization Oktiabr', to be recognized by the party as the sole legitimate voice of Soviet literature. The party rejected their appeal not as incorrect but merely as premature, indicating in the resolution that "leadership in the field of literature belongs to the the working class as a whole, with all its material and ideological resources." This kind of language, overlooked by those writers who viewed the resolution as a defeat for the proletarian faction, paved the way for the concerted attacks on the Fellow Travelers in 1929 and for the party's imposition of complete control over literature at that time.[19] A number of writers understood the dangerous implications of the resolution, however—Sobol, Novikov, Veresaev and Pasternak, to name a few. Pasternak commented that the Soviet Union was undergoing not a cultural revolution, but a cultural reaction[20]—an opinion echoed by Shklovsky in *Third Factory*. The Party Resolution of June 1925, more than anything else, shaped the despairing mood that runs through *Third Factory*, for it showed Shklovsky once and for all that *Opoyaz*, the movement which he had founded and nurtured, was doomed.

The pressures generated by these developments were extreme. Shklovsky apparently tried to write a conciliatory book, but that was not the book which emerged. In that respect, *Third Factory* illustrates a principle discussed often, here and elsewhere, by Shklovsky and many others: that a writer often begins his book with a certain idea in mind, but at some critical point in the writing process, the characters and situations acquire a momentum of their own that dictates the remainder of the book and causes it to swerve. At the end, the writer is left with a manuscript that deviates sharply from his inital idea of what he wanted to do. Shklovsky ruefully described the phenomenon as follows:

> After *Zoo, or Letters Not about Love* I wrote *Third Factory*, a book completely incomprehensible to me. In that book I wanted to capitulate to the time—not only capitulate, but take my troops over to the other side. I wanted to come to terms with the present. As it turned out, however, I had no say in the matter. Both the material on the village and the material on my own disordered state in life, included in the book, got out of hand and acquired a shape contrary to my original plan, so the book was resented. On the whole, however, books are not written to please; in fact, sometimes books are not written: they emerge, they happen. I write this not to vindicate myself but to present a fact.[21]

In *Third Factory*, the contradictions are even more abundant than in *Zoo, or Letters Not about Love,* but the rhythm is essentially the same. Every perfunctory attempt to acquiesce in the literary policies of the regime is immediately undermined and canceled by a defiant statement defending the tenets of *Opoyaz* and the need for creative freedom. The conciliatory statements, like the declarations in *Zoo, or Letters Not about Love* about avoiding the love theme, are always felt as perfunctory and forced. The net effect, then, as Shklovsky's opponents correctly discerned at the time, was a book riddled with defiance. It is anything but the book that "destroyed Formalism." In its total effect, *Third Factory* is a passionate defense of Formalism.

The nature of Shklovsky's defiance can be seen in his treatment of the cherished Marxist slogan "Objective reality determines consciousness" ("Bytie opredeliaet soznanie"). The third chapter of *Third Factory* is called "I Write about How Objective Reality Determines Consciousness . . ."—obviously the right kind of topic for a repentant Formalist, but the last part of the title undermines the first part—"While the Conscience Remains in Disarray." Shklovsky mocks this slogan again in his "Letter to Boris Eikhenbaum":

> As far as objective reality goes, it certainly does determine consciousness.
> But in art, it often runs counter to consciousness. My brain is busy with the daily grind. The high point of the day is morning tea.
> And that is too bad: some artists shed blood and sperm. Others urinate.
> Net weight is all that matters to the buyer.

Once again, the first sentence is a concession, but the sentence that follows immediately retracts the concession. And the letter concludes with Shklovsky's bitter reaction to the fact that the new society places no value on the work of *Opoyaz.*

The nominal theme of acquiescence in *Third Factory* centers on the word "time." Shklovsky states repeatedly that he wants to understand his time and to respond to it in his writing. He comments that in the old days (the second factory), he viewed art as an autonomous system and concerned himself with

xvi

freedom, whereas now he is making a study of unfreedom. Yet these statements are contradicted everywhere in the book and are finally overpowered. In the previously mentioned chapter on objective reality and the conscience, for example, he says that he wants to speak with his time and understand its voice. Then he observes:

> But chance is crucial to art. The dimensions of a book have always been dictated to an author.
> The marketplace gave a writer his voice.
> A work of literature lives on material. *Don Quixote* and *The Minor* owe their existence to unfreedom.
> It is impossible to exclude certain material: necessity creates works of literature. I need the freedom to work from my own plans; freedom is needed if the material is to be bared. I don't want to be told that I have to make bentwood chairs out of rocks.

He concludes by saying that the members of *Opoyaz* are not cowards—they love the wind of the revolution. And he insists that he be allowed to cultivate his own garden, since it is wrong for everyone to sow wheat. He is unable to squeak like the toy elephant; besides, it is wrong to coddle art.

From this passage, it becomes evident that in talking about unfreedom or necessity, Shklovsky is not talking about the civic responsibility of the writer in Soviet society. The statement, in its abstract form, sounds acceptable to the demands of the Marxist critics, but Shklovsky has obliquely defined the term "freedom" in terms of pressure of the material (the same pressures that led to the creation of *Don Quixote*). In this way, then, he concludes that the writer in fact needs freedom to respond to the material of his time as he perceives it—the writer must not be made to write according to formulas dictated by the government.

This approach is also seen, with particular clarity, in the chapter "On the Freedom of Art," where Shklovsky says that he wants freedom and that a writer requires the illusion of choice. An artist, he says, cannot be ordered to praise phenomena, as the peasants are now being made to do. Still, he says in apparent contradiction, "that doesn't mean that we need freedom of art. Lev Tolstoy would not have written *War and Peace* had he not been a gunner." The illustration, once again, supplies a special definition that deprives the abstract statement of its conciliatory import. An artist is bound to respond to his experience in writing his books. The artist, however, must be free to respond to that experience as he perceives it. Tolstoy, says Shklovsky, "like many others" (!), tried to espouse a utilitarian theory of art, but "The works that resulted were completely different. Art processes the ethics and world view of a writer and liberates itself from his original intention. Things change when they land in a book." Here Shklovsky has widened his original definition in a way that makes his idea of unfreedom even more heretical: the artist is unfree in the sense that he must respond to his own experience and perceptions *and* he is also unfree in the sense that he must respond to the dictates of form, a variant of Shklovsky's old idea that form determines content. Finally, Shklovsky offers what at first glance seems to be a recognition of the hard realities, but this acquiescence is then converted into a refusal to recognize those realities. The passage ends with notes of open protest about the treatment of unorthodox artists:

At the moment, there are two alternatives. To retreat, dig in, earn a living outside literature and write at home for oneself.

The other alternative is to have a go at describing life, to conscientiously seek out the new society and the correct world view.

There is no third alternative. Yet that is precisely the one that must be chosen. An artist should avoid beaten paths.

The third alternative is to work in newspapers and journals every day, to be unsparing of yourself and caring about the work, to change, to crossbreed with the material, change some more, crossbreed with the material, process it some more—and then there will be literature.

In the life of Pushkin, the one clearly unnecessary thing was D'Anthes' bullet.

But terror and oppression are necessary.

A strange business. The poor flax.

You see, the artist doesn't produce an orderly arrangement of happiness. He produces a product.

This last sentence tersely reasserts a position that Shklovsky is supposedly abandoning in *Third Factory:* that art is primarily form, not content. This point is made at greater length in the "Letter to Tynyanov," where Shklovsky insists on a wide range of options for the writer that few Marxists would endorse:

> Literature stays alive by expanding into non-literature. But artistic form carries out its own unique rape of the Sabine women. The material ceases to recognize its former lord and master. It is processed by the law of art and can now be perceived apart from its place of origin. If that makes no sense, try this explanation. With regard to real life, art possesses several freedoms: 1) the freedom of non-recognition, 2) the freedom of choice, 3) the freedom of absorption (a fact long gone in life may be preserved in art). Art converts the particularity of things into perceptible form.

Shklovsky concludes this letter with another theoretical discussion that sounds as though he will now demonstrate the sincerity of his repudiation of Formalism. He admits in the proper fashion that both he and Eikhenbaum have failed to give proper consideration to non-esthetic norms. He then implicitly reverses himself by condemning Eikhenbaum for attempting to follow that very course: the exploration of non-esthetic norms in his book *The Young Tolstoi* (1923):

> It is also a serious mistake to use diaries to explain the way a work of literature comes into being. There is a hidden lie here—as though a writer creates and writes all by himself and not in conjunction with his genre and all of literature, with all its conflicting tendencies. Writing a monograph on a writer is an impossible task. Moreover, diaries lead us into the psychology of the creative process and the question of the laboratory of the genius, when what we need is the thing. The relation between the thing and its creator is also nonfunctional. With regard to the writer, art has three freedoms: 1) the freedom to

xix

ignore his personality, 2) the freedom to choose from his personality, 3) the freedom to choose from any other material whatsoever. One must study not the problematical connection, but the facts. One must write not about Tolstoy, but about *War and Peace*.

Surely no one would argue that these passages demonstrate Shklovsky's conversion to the Marxist view of literature. Surely it is a serious error to maintain that *Third Factory* "destroyed Formalism."

In the last chapter of the book, Shklovsky speaks about his work in the film industry, referring to the room where unsuccessful films are stored as a kind of cemetery. He says that in a time of film famine, the dead buried in that cemetery will be resurrected. Then the range of reference widens with the chilling reproach, "But never will the dead buried in our cemeteries be resurrected." The chapter concludes with a citation from Virgil: "And the southern wind, / With a quiet creaking of the masts, / Calls us to the open sea." This line occurs in the *Aeneid* at that point where the survivors of shattered Troy, leaving the dead and dying of the city behind them, have set forth with the hope of preserving their culture in another land. The parallels between fallen Troy and fallen Petersburg, also used by Shklovsky in *Zoo, or Letters Not about Love*, need no comment. They are sustained even by the desperate hope that Shklovsky expresses in this chapter and elsewhere in the book: "We must not die: kindred spirits will be found."

The heresies embedded in every nook and cranny of *Third Factory* did not escape the attention of Shklovsky's detractors, who were numerous and eager for blood. Gorky—from his faraway place in Sorrento, of course—complained about the unhealthy mood of the book.[22] The critic Abram Lezhnev spoke scornfully of Shklovsky as "that posturing Hamlet of *Opoyaz*, ready at a moment's notice to change into a self-abnegating Don Quixote." He observed that, despite verbal camouflage, Shklovsky remained partisan to his old and most serious heresy: the dichotomy of art and life. Lezhnev concluded that "despite some moments that approached Marxism, Shklovsky basically remains true to his old positions."[23]

That is an accurate assessment of the book.

Most serious of all, though, was the campaign mounted in March, 1927, by the influential proletarian critic Osip Beskin, who was director of the literary division of Gosizdat. The main point made by Beskin in his attacks on the book was that Shklovsky was the most reactionary figure on the Soviet literary scene—an extremely dangerous influence whose true purposes had been discerned, though he, like a fox, tried to cover his tracks with his tail. Beskin also describes him as a "refined literary gentleman mocking his 'uncouth reader.' " Particularly seditious, in Beskin's opinion, is the pun in "Envy Bay," where the audience reminds Solovei that there will certainly be no match shortage after NEP begins. Then someone says, "They'll be spared an NEP. They hold their fire" ("U nikh ne budet [NEP]. Oni beregut ogon' "). Such an irreverent attitude toward the civil war was offensive to Beskin. Equally offensive to him were those places in the book where Shklovsky explicitly displays his hostility to Marxism. Here Beskin feels that Shklovsky shows his true colors—as a passively hostile element whose views are corrupting the literary theory and art of the new era.[24] The main points of this attack had been made earlier in the month by Beskin at a symposium held to evaluate the role of a reorganized LEF in Soviet society.

Shklovsky's book provided welcome ammunition for the proletarian writers in their attempts to discredit LEF, and it seems clear that Shklovsky would have been in serious trouble if Mayakovsky had not come to his defense. When Beskin insisted on the arch-reactionary and dangerous nature of Shklovsky's views, Mayakovsky admitted that there were many unfortunate things in the book, but insisted that Shklovsky's energies and talents were needed by Soviet society and that LEF was attempting to rehabilitate Shklovsky. He remarked that, had LEF been responsible for the publication of the book, its members would have persuaded Shklovsky to make changes. Mayakovsky mentions that the book was published with the approval of Voronsky, who was one of the supervisors of the "Krug" publishing house. The implication is that Voronsky, who was generally hostile to Shklovsky, let the book be published in its unexpurgated form in order to expose Shklovsky to calumny.[25]

It is true, as Beskin observed, that Shklovsky sometimes takes issue with the Marxists openly, but the most telling criticism of the regime is lodged in the cryptic imagery of the book. In no other book has Shklovsky relied so heavily on figurative language. The following extended image is an oblique way of complaining about the regimentation of literature.

> An oyster draws the valves of its shell together with a supreme effort. Having drawn them shut, it stops functioning. Its muscles no longer radiate heat, but they do hold the valves shut.
> Prose and poetry are being held in such a death grip. Muscles warm and living could never exert the necessary force.
> Thirty-three-year-old shell, I am sick today. I know how heavy is the force that keeps the valves together. That should not be.

Central to the meaning of the book are three images which recur and interlock: a toy elephant, a Tolstoian anecdote about a butcher sharpening his knife on cobblestones, and flax, all subjected to constant modulation. All three images are used to demonstrate Shklovsky's resistance to the official line and his ultimate refusal to acquiesce in the liquidation of *Opoyaz*. The opposition expressed in the figurative language of these images substantially reinforces the open expressions of dissent already mentioned. Together, they overwhelm and cancel out Shklovsky's nominal attempt to accede to the demands of his time.

The elephant image leans heavily on the word "voice." Shklovsky begins the book by saying that he speaks in a voice hoarse from silence and feuilletons. Then he evokes his infant son, playing with a toy elephant that squeaks when pressed. "We are cranked out in various shapes," says Shklovsky in an oblique reference to government pressure, "but we speak in one voice when pressure is applied."

The image, once established, is used as a reference point throughout the early part of the book. After expressing doubts about his current situation, Shklovsky says, "That's not the elephant squeaking—that is my voice." Then he gives a mock apology for his individualistic views, for the fact that he does not know how to speak in an elephant squeak.

In Tolstoy's anecdote, an observer notices a young man from the meat counter who seems to be doing something to the stones in the sidewalk. Upon closer inspection, he finds that the man is doing nothing at all to the stones: he is doing something to a knife—sharpening it on the stones. Shklovsky adapts this anecdote in the following way. He says that in art, what matters is the sharpening of the knife. The stones are secondary. In this oblique way, he expresses the view that he has supposedly abandoned: That esthetic norms (the knife) are independent of extra-esthetic norms (the stones). What matters in art is the process, as Shklovsky says explicitly in his letter to Eikhenbaum.

In the letter to Brik, criticizing him for not finishing his book on verse structure, Shklovsky emphasizes his point with figurative language drawn from the anecdote: "Brik," he says, "feels no urge to cut, so he refuses to sharpen the knife." The anecdote is also used in the chapter "About the Second Factory," where Shklovsky praises Eikhenbaum's article on Gogol's "Overcoat":

> The meat was cut well—that means we sharpened the knife properly.
> Don't tell us who we are. We are the stones on which the truth is sharpened.

Here the image is modulated. The stones are equated not with extra-esthetic norms, but with artists.

Interwoven with the elephant and the knife images, and similar in import, is the flax image, which becomes the metaphoric axis of the book. Shklovsky worked at a flax center after his return to the Soviet Union and became sufficiently expert on flax cultivation to criticize Gorky's novel *The Artamanovs' Business* for its many inaccuracies in this regard.[26]

Shklovsky establishes this dominant metaphor at the beginning of the chapter called "The Voice of a Semiprocessed Commodity," where he says, "We are flax in the field." By "We," he means those artists and critics resistant to the demands for conformity—in particular, he means the members of *Opoyaz*.

This becomes abundantly clear where he says, "And let me cultivate my own garden. It's wrong for everyone to sow wheat. I am unable to squeak like the elephant." Subsequently, he refers to Mayakovsky as top-grade flax and describes the rude treatment he is receiving in the press by using the special verbs that describe how flax is processed. Elsewhere Shklovsky wonders despairingly whether the members of *Opoyaz* were sown for fiber or for seed.

One of the most interesting and extended uses of this metaphor appears in the previously mentioned chapter called "About the Freedom of Art." There, in speaking about the processing of flax, Shklovsky clearly has in mind the inevitable fate of unorthodox elements:

> FLAX. This is no advertisement. I'm not employed at the Flax Center these days. At the moment, I'm more interested in pitch. In tapping trees to death. That is how turpentine is obtained.
>
> From the tree's point of view, it is ritual murder.
> The same with flax.
> Flax, if it had a voice, would shriek as it's being processed. It is taken by the head and jerked from the ground. By the root. It is sown thickly—oppressed, so that it will be not vigorous but puny.
> Flax requires oppression. It is jerked out of the ground, spread out on the fields (in some places) or retted in pits and streams.
> The streams where the flax is washed are doomed—the fish disappear. Then the flax is braked and scutched.
> I want freedom.

One of the recurrent images in *Third Factory* is vegetable soup. Concealed in this image is a polemic with the previously mentioned Lunacharsky. In an article printed in 1924, Lunacharsky had said, "Before October, formalism was simply a vegetable in season. Now it is a living relic of the past—a palladium where those elements of the intelligentsia oriented toward bourgeois Europe are making their last stand."[27]

This image is introduced in the chapter on Doctor Kulbin,

where Shklovsky says, "Now that the volcanoes have stopped erupting, the soup has come to a boil and is being poured into various bowls." He continues this motif in the chapters on Osip Brik:

> The earthquake is over. The lid has been removed, the soup has come to a boil, the spoons have been distributed. "Help yourself," they say.
> We have the right to refuse the spoons.
> We are, after all, the "ideological superstructure."
> The connection between us and the soup is complicated and non-functional.

The identity of the cooks is obvious. And one would hardly describe Shklovsky's reaction to the dinner invitation as abject surrender. The spoons are refused. A favorite Marxist cliché is mocked. And the existence of a relationship between art and society is denied. This image is further developed several lines later, where the confrontation becomes more direct:

> Vegetables, for example, are sometimes cooked in soup and then discarded.
> It is essential, though, to understand what happens in that process. Otherwise, you can get the story wrong and mistake noise for work.
> Noise is work for an orchestra, but not for the Putilov plant.
> On the whole, we probably were vegetables.
> But not according to the reading from our meridian.
> And I—gazing at the samplers from Turkestan, stuffing the silk pillows behind the couch, smudging the upholstery with my leather pants, devouring everything on the table—I was cooked along with the others at the Briks.

Now the terms of the image have shifted. The reluctant guests at the feast have become the ingredients—used for flavoring and then discarded. Shklovsky has ridiculed Lunacharsky's statement by the technique of the realized metaphor—by treating the vegetable reference literally and then dilating the image until it explodes. Included in the passage just cited is a good example of the accommodation retraction pattern:

> On the whole, we probably were vegetables.
> But not according to the reading from our meridian.

The final occurrence of this particular image is also the most famous—the most defiant. In the chapter called "A Case Ineptly Pleaded by Me," Shklovsky says, "We are not Marxists, but if that utensil should prove useful in our household, we will not eat with our hands out of spite." This statement still rankled in certain circles three years later. The Marxist critic Isaak Nusinov, gloating over the beleaguered Shklovsky, wrote a scathing review of Shklovsky's book *Material and Style in Lev Tolstoi's Novel "War and Peace."* The review was entitled, "Belated Discoveries, or How V. Shklovsky Got Tired of Eating with His Bare Formalist Hands and so Supplied Himself with a Homemade Marxist Spoon."[28]

Shklovsky's witticism cropped up again in an interesting dispute between Kornely Zelinsky, leader of the Constructivist Movement, and Ivan Grossman-Roshchin, a leader of the proletarian writers. Complaining about conditions in the Soviet Union, Zelinsky said that the emphasis on rationality made life dull, sober and joyless. He also objected to the idea of sacrificing the present on the altar of a glorious future. "Man should not be fertilizer for the future. I do not want a life in the antechamber of some future palace. My life is here and now." Accordingly, he advocated the establishment of a Bank of Public Confidence, where people could cash checks giving them the right to a "full-blooded, joyous, merry, devil-may-care existence."

Grossman-Roshchin, refusing Zelinsky the glamour of a comparison to the Underground Man, called him a capitalist, a spiritual emigre and a rebel with the sniffles. He continued by saying that Zelinsky didn't want to cook the soup of the future—he wanted to eat it right away. "As we know," said Grossman-Roshchin, "the Shklovskys of this world recommend that people not pick up the October spoons, because the interrelation between them and the October soup is an extremely complicated one!"[29]

The images which have been discussed, for all their variety, point to underlying assumptions highly critical of the government's attitudes toward unorthodox elements. If Marx spoke about how bourgeois society treated the worker as a commodity, Shklovsky is saying that the new society is treating writers as commodities—semiperishable, or even expendable commodities: a toy elephant to be squeezed, vegetables to be cooked, flax to be uprooted, soaked and crushed—a crop not wanted in a society where everyone must plant wheat. He speaks of himself and friends as merchandise to be picked over and probably discarded by the dominant proletarian class. The section devoted to village life suggests that the peasants too are being treated as commodities—a suggestion most explicit in the chapter called "Cheap Motors," which is a metaphor for peasant girls.

The critical attitude moored in these images is also found in "Envy Bay," an exercise in the *skaz* form. "Envy Bay" illustrates Shklovsky's conception of the *skaz*, as expressed in his "Letter to Eikhenbaum," and shows the nature of their disagreement. Shklovsky feels that Eikhenbaurn exaggerates the importance of oral coloration. For Shklovsky, the *skaz* is a plot device that affords an opportunity to play with point of view. Here he plays with the interaction between two speech events. In accordance with his "flicker effect," in which illusion is created, then dissolved, he constantly breaches the integrity of the two speech events by the use of a hyperbolic and volatile form—by "laying bare" the devices of the *skaz,* by distorting its proportions, and by establishing scenes and characters, then eliminating them.

The inner narrative of "Envy Bay" concerns a Russian ship dispatched to discover a tropical island and name it after the Tsarina Catherine's new lover, Count Mordvinkin. The sailors find an island, befriend the natives, and marvel at their customs—a situation which motivates ironic comments on censorship and intervention, as well as comparisons with Russian customs during the NEP period. The natives, like the Russians, lack matches. The natives use mats for money instead of the food rations which the Russians use. The natives wear only bracelets, while the Russians cavort in their public baths. Strangest of all, the natives do not beat women and show consideration for each other. Life on the island is so attractive to the sailors that they remain with the natives.

Shklovsky encloses this inner narrative in a complicated frame. In Petrograd, during the cold winter of 1919, a strange assortment of characters meets in a room over an antique shop called "The Cheerful Native." The characters, completely schematic, include the owner of the shop and narrator of the inner narrative, Nightingale; his friend, Jack the Witless; a nondescript, irrelevant woman named Rosa, introduced toward the end of the *skaz* purely as a violation of its proportions; and a first-person narrator, who functions both as a character in the frame and as the author of the whole *skaz*. He periodically interrupts Nightingale's story about the Russian sailors to ask questions and to comment on the technical features of the *skaz*.

As Nightingale finishes telling the inner narrative, the characters in the frame admit that they have no passes and speculate on how to return home without being stopped by patrols. The *skaz* concludes with a neat circular ending—a reprise of the motifs of the story about the Russian sailors and a new motif that links the inner narrative with the frame: when the Russian sailors fail to return, Count Mordvinkin receives instead of his island a set of china, now on sale at "The Cheerful Native."

"Envy Bay" begins with several false starts—comments on different ways of catching fish and a digression about the old French houses that were built with special passageways for cats. The first-person narrator walks to the antique shop to see Nightingale. The characters huddle under a fur coat in Nightingale's room as he begins the inner narrative about the Russian sailors.

Before the digression on French cats, the narrator, speaking as author, abruptly remarks that he has forgotten to straighten out the coordinates of time and space in the story. Without doing so, he proceeds to the digression. Then he mentions the coordinates again and announces, in defiance of the characters shivering under a fur coat in the dead of winter, that the time is May. This toying with fictional time conventions continues as he walks on May 1 to see Nightingale in his freezing room. Then in rapid succession, he cancels the cold, reaffirms May, and returns to winter:

> On that day, however, it wasn't cold; I touched up this
> passage with cold by mistake.
> It was May.
> Let's begin at the beginning.
> Not with the cat, of course. It was winter.

Nightingale begins telling the story—how the Russian
sailors talked about the French Revolution and women as they
sailed across the Pacific. At this point, the first-person narrator,
speaking as author, announces that he is scratching out these
conversations. Similar establishment and cancelation occur with
one of the characters of the story—the boatswain. Nightingale
relates that the boatswain stays on board because he is a *skopets*.
The first-person narrator suggests that this scene be scratched
out. Nightingale then changes the motivation: the boatswain
stays on board out of fidelity to his wife. Then the boatswain is
reported as criticizing the profligate behavior of the sailors on
shore. The first-person narrator apologizes for his unsuccessful
deletion and for the reappearance of the boatswain.

Shklovsky also hyperbolizes imagery in this *skaz*. In the
following passage, he plays with colors, which include a gray
cat. Then he transfers an attribute of the cat to the foam of the
waves. Then he realizes the image of the white foam until it
explodes:

> The cannons sprayed sunbeams and threw golden
> sparklers on the sails.
> The black sides of the frigate boiled like pitch.
> A gray cat, trying to run across the molten deck, squeaked
> and licked its burned paws with a dry tongue.
> The white tail of the foam, held high, ran alongside the
> rudder of the ship.
> A white belt.
> White foam, scraggly as a bear, and chrysanthemums,
> shaggy as the sheepdog in Pokrovsky-Streshnyov, wrapped
> around the island.
> The wreath hissed and crackled, paying no attention to the

ship flying the tsar's flag.

The foam, curving, pursued the frigate.

The frigate circled the islands; for a minute, a strait appeared, but the white wreath hissed and crackled.

The question of how to describe surf without lapsing into literary clichés was raised by Shklovsky in *Zoo, or Letters Not about Love*. Elsa Triolet had written him a letter (no. 21) in which she described the surf off Tahiti as making foam that formed a "gigantic, white, imperishable garland (*venok*)." In Letter no. 23, Shklovsky gently criticized the excessively literary nature of her description. In "Envy Bay," he demonstrates a type of enstrangement that can solve the problem of describing foam and the wreath (*venok*) that it makes around an island: he avoids inert adjectives, relying instead on unusual, down-to-earth images and on unusual verbs.

Throughout the first half of 1927, Shklovsky was subjected to critical abuse for the heresies of *Third Factory*. The climate in which he lived made him recall wistfully the days of the revolution and the possibilities for freedom of expression that had since been limited: "Then there was no need for the grief of structuring life and restoring it. Only the carbohydrates and proteins were lacking to strengthen the kingdom of intellectual freedom under the cannons of Aurora."[30]

In 1928, Shklovsky received a hard blow from an unexpected quarter. Venyamin Kaverin published a satirical novel in which he mercilessly exposed the peccadilloes of his former mentor. In this novel, entitled *The Troublemaker, or Evenings on Vasily Island*,[31] Kaverin depicted Shklovsky in the transparent guise of Professor Nekrylov, a disoriented egoist clinging desperately to the remnants of his former eminence.

Nekrylov works in the Moscow film industry, but he frequently visits his old literary associates in Leningrad. There he sharpens his notorious wit on friends as well as enemies, indulges in venial love affairs, and goads young writers with outrageous declarations. In his books and in all his activities, he aims only to publicize himself:

Meanwhile he was managing to arrange an easy life. It

would have been still easier if he were not making such a fuss about the creation of his historical role. He did have a role in history, but he had overplayed it in articles, feuilletons, and letters. The role had worn thin. It had begun to seem that he did not have it. All the same, he was always ready to enter into history without paying the least attention to whether he was invited or not.[32]

Throughout the novel, Kaverin makes Nekrylov pontificate on themes identified with Shklovsky, such as the need for a new kind of literature. Nekrylov is always insisting lugubriously on the need to capitulate to the time, one of the central themes of *Third Factory*. In one scene, Nekrylov proudly tells a group of young writers about the Hottentots who told time from a burning tree—an allusion to "Envy Bay" in *Third Factory*.

In the last scene of the novel, Nekrylov wonders whether he should renounce irony—an obvious allusion to Shklovsky's dilemma in the mid-twenties. In a passage replete with ironic references to *Third Factory*, Nekrylov muses: "And to be precise—it is better to lie down in a safe than to be an ensign who thinks that the whole squad is out of step and only he is in step. And to be precise—it is better to go to Persia than, as in *The Decameron*, to tell stories in order to avert the plague. The time which had crushed him was right."[33]

Kaverin eventually described the genesis of this novel:

> During the winter of 1928, I often met at Yury Tynyanov's place a lively and clever writer then at the zenith of his powers and deeply convinced that he knew all the mysteries of the literature business. We spoke about the novel genre, and the writer observed that since even Chekhov could not cope with this genre, no wonder it was not succeeding in contemporary literature. I objected, and he, with the irony at which he was always unusually adept, expressed doubts about my abilities in this complex business. Infuriated, I said that I would launch a novel and that it would be a book about him—about a troublemaker who conducted his whole life with an awareness of his literary role. He derided me—but to no avail. On the very next day, I began to write the novel *The Troublemaker, or*

Evenings on Vasily Island. Obviously, only youth is capable of such decisions, and only in youth could you so openly follow at the heels of your future character with a notebook. He laughed at me: "the utilitarian Kaverin factory." I jotted even that down. He spouted jokes, made brilliant witticisms, sometimes unusually well directed and remembered for a lifetime—I blushed, but jotted them down. Probably, he was fully convinced that nothing would come of the novel; otherwise, he would have been more cautious in this unusual due.[34]

The imposition of the First Five-Year Plan in 1928 quickly brought an end to the movements with which Shklovsky had been identified. The Serapion Brothers ceased to be a viable entity. The vicious campaign against the leaders of the Fellow Travelers, Evgeny Zamyatin and Boris Pilnyak, in 1929 made clear that the time of tolerating elements not actively supportive of the Party had passed. RAPP, the new organization of the Proletarian writers, was now delegated the power over literary affairs that it had sought in 1925.

During the same year, the New LEF, deprived of Mayakovsky's support, dissolved—an event that Shklovsky has sadly described as the "passing of the last literary salon in Russia."[35] The desperate attempts of the Formalists to find a compromise satisfactory to the Marxist critics remained unsuccessful. Shklovsky's attempts to create a synthesis of the sociological method and the Formal Method were greeted with derision.[36]

In early January of 1930, another hard blow fell. The critic Grigory Gukovsky published a devastating review of Shklovsky's most recent attempt at a methodological compromise—*Matvei Komarov, Inhabitant of the City of Moscow.*[37] This article was not the vicious personal attack to which Shklovsky had become accustomed, but a rigorous dissection of his study, point by point.

A few weeks later, Shklovsky published "A Monument to Scientific Error," the "third surrender"of the trilogy and the work which is uniformly viewed as Shklovsky's total capitulation to the regime. According to this view, there were two alternatives for the Formalists by 1930: to become silent or to acknowledge their errors; and Shklovsky, the most aggressive and "presumably the most intransigent" of the group, was the first to recant the doctrines of *Opoyaz* publicly. According to Professor Erlich, this was not too surprising, since "the *enfant terrible* of Formalism had started losing his nerve rather early," as seen in *Zoo, or Letters Not about Love,* his first recantation:

> Gone were the days when Shklovsky referred airily to Marxism as a gadget which might someday come in handy, when he wrote that "dialectical materialism is a very fine thing for a sociologist, but no substitute for a knowledge of mathematics and astronomy." Now he was quite ready to swear by the name of the master and to recognize Marxist dialectics as the alpha and omega of literary scholarship. "Sociological dilettantism," he wrote in the concluding passage, "simply will not do. It is necessary to undertake a thorough study of the Marxist method in its entirety."[38]

A close look at "Monument," however, reveals that silence or open recantation were not the only two alternatives available in 1930. To adapt Shklovsky's heretical remark in *Third Factory,* there was no third alternative, but that was precisely the one that he chose. The third choice was the device of ostensible surrender, the device canonized in *Third Factory*—outward obedience undermined by defiance. The title of the article refers to a novel by Jules Romains called *Donogoo Tonka.*[39] In that book, a famous geographer faces the possibility that he will be denied membership in the Academy of Sciences because his most noted work contains a map of South America showing a city named Donogoo Tonka that does not exist. Through a series of hilarious and improbable events, the error is rectified by the hasty construction of a city with that name and the geographer is elected to the Academy. The book ends with the official promulgation in Donogoo Tonka of a cult of scientific error, to which the city owes its existence, and an appropriate statue is erected.

Shklovsky says in his article that he has no desire to stand as a monument to his own error. He admits that anyone ignoring the effect of the class struggle on literature is thereby neutralizing certain sectors of the front and he admits that his approach to literature in the early twenties was too narrow, but insists that he and the Formalists have long since modified those early positions. He mentions that Eikhenbaum had performed a useful service by urging the substitution of the term "morphological method" for "formal method." In particular, he mentions the contribution of Tynyanov, whose article on the literary fact, published in 1924 and dedicated to Shklovsky, criticized the view of literature as a static sum of devices and offered the proposition that a work of literature is a network of devices with complicated and dynamic interrelationships that change with the passage of time—a view whose value Shklovsky had recognized immediately, as his letter to Tynyanov in *Third Factory* proves. He also mentions his study of *War and Peace* and his book on Matvei Komarov, both of which demonstrate new approaches to literature. He complains specifically that people have continued to charge the Formalists with the defects of their initial period and have refused to take into account the fact that they have long since abandoned those positions of their own accord.

Shklovsky's article, then, was not a betrayal of the Formalists, but a defense of their position as it had evolved during the twenties. Here, as in *Third Factory*, one can gain a false impression of the article when only the conciliatory passages are quoted without the subsequent remarks that undermine them. Without those remarks, his article sounds like a complete denunciation of Formalism accompanied by a meek acceptance of the Marxist point of view. However, it is instructive to look at the concluding portion of the article in its entirety:

> People still think of the formal method in terms of its initial stage, when the elementary propositions were being defined, the material was being selected, and the terminology was becoming established.
>
> As far as I am concerned, Formalism is a road already traversed—traversed and left several stages behind. The most important stage was the shift to consideration of the function of literary form. The only thing left of the Formal Method is the terminology, now being used by everyone, and a series of observations of a technological nature.
>
> But for studying literary evolution on the social plane, the

crude sociological approach is absolutely worthless.

It is essential to turn to the study of the Marxist method in its entirety.

It goes without saying that I am not declaring myself a Marxist, because one does not adhere to scientific methods. One masters them and one creates them.[40]

This final paragraph echoes the statement made by Shklovsky in his "Letter to Lev Yakubinsky," where he tells his friend that he is "not about to become a hard-and-fast Marxist" and advises him to follow his example. Shklovsky is not repudiating Formalism in "Monument" and he is certainly not adhering to Marxism: his strategy is to redefine the word "Formalism" so that it applies exclusively to the initial period of the movement, say, from 1914 to 1923. He freely admits the limitations of the approach taken then, but strongly defends the positions evolved by the movement since 1923. As the quotation shows, he is not enthusiastic about the sociological approach and his attitude toward the Marxist method is made equivocal by the puzzling qualification "in its entirety." And equivocation becomes subtle repudiation not buried in the text or couched in cryptic riddles, but stated openly and offered as the final thought. Shklovsky explicitly refuses to declare himself a Marxist. The grounds for his refusal? Humility—a trait most people had previously overlooked in his personality. He will need time to master the scientific methods perfected by the Marxists. But this is Shklovsky speaking—the founder of an approach to literature that sought above all else to be scientific. In *Third Factory* ("Evenings at the Briks"), he outlined the essence of the formal method as a systematic approach to art, the refusal to view it as a reflection. He said, "We located the distinctive features of the genus. We began defining the basic tendencies of form. We understood that, in fact, you can distill from works of literature the homogeneous laws that determine their shape. In short, science is possible." In the context of the statements supporting the formal approach and attacking the Marxist approach that Shklovsky made throughout the twenties, the reason given for his refusal to declare himself a Marxist in 1930 can be viewed only as irony, if not sarcasm.

After a close examination of Shklovsky's article, it is difficult to endorse the following statement: "With the fiery champion of *Opoyaz* declaring Formalism to be a thing of the past, the remaining Formalist spokesmen had no other choice but to acquiesce in their own extinction. Whatever their reaction to Shklovsky's statement, they were in no position to disassociate themselves publicly from it."

Yet Shklovsky's article did not strike all the critics as an epitaph to Formalism and a subservient acceptance of Marxist dialectics. M. Gelfand, in an article called "The Declaration of Tsar Midas, or What Has Happened to Viktor Shklovsky,"[42] accused Shklovsky of attempting a vicious maneuver designed to salvage the Formal Method, which required complete extinction. He accused him of attempting to deceive the Soviet public, taking particular umbrage at Shklovsky's phrase "neutralization of certain sectors of the front," which he identified as "a euphemism for vicious ideological sabotage, conducted at the behest of the bourgeoisie." He went on to suggest ominously "the absolute neutralization of the neutralizers by an ideological firing squad." Gelfand answered his own question repeatedly: nothing has happened to Viktor Shklovsky; he remains committed to his previous views. Shklovsky defended himself in an article entitled "Fish out of Water, or Equation with an Unknown Quantity," which he published at the end of March. He scoffed at Gelfand's charges and announced his intention to continue pursuing his work:

> What do I do?
> I swim in the sea and behold new stars, understanding the laws of their movement anew.
> The fish out of water will not catch me.[43]

The unconditional surrender sought by Shklovsky's enemies, in fact, never came, despite the savage campaign against him provoked by "Monument." Where this campaign would have ended is difficult to say. It was eclipsed two weeks later by the suicide of Mayakovsky, which shook the literary world of the Soviet Union profoundly and which was an intensely felt personal tragedy for Shklovsky, whom

Mayakovsky had rescued from difficult situations many times.

Those who treat "Monument" as Shklovsky's final capitulation create the impression that thereafter he submitted meekly to the party line in order to survive and publish.[44] This is not the place to embark on a study of Shklovsky's career after 1930, but even a cursory examination of that period reveals a completely different sort of pattern. Far from "playing it safe," Shklovsky continued throughout the thirties and forties to salvage what he could of the legacy left by *Opoyaz*. During the breathing space between the creation of the Writers' Union in 1932 and the First Congress of Soviet Writers in 1934, he produced extremely interesting articles on such controversial figures as Olesha, Mandelstam, Tynyanov and Eisenstein. *Literaturnaia gazeta* was charged with irresponsiblity for allowing such "formalistically oriented" work to appear on its pages, and the first edition of the *Large Soviet Encyclopedia,* referring to the articles of this period, described them as "based on the false concepts of Formalism."[45]

In 1933, Shklovsky was attacked for his article "Southwest," which, among other heresies, overemphasized the influence of the West on the Odessa school of writers.[46] During the massive campaign against experimental art and "Formalism" in 1936 and 1937, he was called to task once again for the continuing pernicious effect of his ideas.

In 1940, Shklovsky published his book on Mayakovsky, the product of his preoccupation with the fate of the poet throughout the thirties. This book was denounced by the Marxist critics for its emphasis on the influence of Futurism and its attempt to rehabilitate the discredited Formalist theories. The hostile reaction to *Mayakovsky* set the stage for a long, difficult period that Shklovsky was lucky to survive. After 1946, it became exceedingly dangerous to stress the role of the West in the development of Russian culture—an idea which had always been foremost in his writing. This campaign against the "cosmopolites" included extremely repressive measures against the Jews. Shklovsky was vulnerable on both counts. It would have been advisable for him to be inconspicuous during this period, but he exacerbated his position by writing a long defense of Veselovsky, who was being attacked as a primary source of contamination from the West.

Between 1948 and 1953, almost nothing written by Shklovsky appeared in print. He reached the nadir of his existence as critic and writer in 1953 with the book *Remarks on the Prose of the Russian Classics,* a dismal product of this difficult period; but in his work since the death of Stalin, he has returned at least partially to his earlier positions and has produced work of high quality.

Even this cursory account suggests how wrong it is to view "Monument" as the capitulation of a once-bold critic and to assume that he adhered to the party line after 1930. The testimony of Nadezhda Mandelstam alone has shown the falsity of that conception of his career. During the most dangerous years of the thirties—even in 1937, a year Russians remember with special dread—such pariahs as the Mandelstams were given shelter by Shklovsky, whose past made such generosity extremely dangerous. As Nadezhda Mandelstam says, "In Moscow there was only one house to which an outcast could always go." That was the house of Viktor and Vasilisa Shklovsky.

RICHARD SHELDON
1977

NOTES

1. Viktor B. Shklovsky, *Zoo, or Letters Not about Love; Zoo, ili pis'ma ne o liubvi* (Berlin, 1923). Censored versions of this edition appeared in the Soviet Union in 1924, 1929, 1964 and 1966, with new letters added and subtracted along the way. For a full account of these changes, see the English translation published by Cornell University Press in 1971 (reprinted by Dalkey Archive Press, 2001).

2. Viktor B. Shklovskii, *Tret'ia fabrika* (M., 1926).

3. Viktor B. Shklovskii, "Pamiatnik nauchnoi oshibke," *Literaturnaia gazeta,* 14 (January 27, 1930), p. 1.

4. For a detailed account of the struggle between these two groups, see K. D. Muratova, *M. Gor'kii v bor'be za sovetskuiu literaturu* (M.-L., 1958), pp. 23-42. See also Sheila Fitzpatrick, *The Commissariat of Enlightenment* (Cambridge, 1970), pp. 113-127.

5. These events are described by Shklovsky in his book *Sentimental'noe puteshestvie. Vospominaniia 1917-1922* (Berlin, 1923). Censored versions were published in the Soviet Union in 1924 and 1929. See the English translation *(A Sentimental Journey)* published by Cornell University Press in 1970.

6. See Maxim Gorky, *Untimely Thoughts,* translated and edited by Herman Ermolaev (New York, 1968). These articles, omitted from Soviet collections of Gorky's work, were published in Gorky's journal *The New Life (Novaia zhizn'),* which Lenin suppressed in July, 1918.

7. See, for example, Brik's provocative statement in the issue dated December 29, 1918: "Many gods have been overthrown by the proletariat, many idols have been overturned. But one god has been spared. The conquering proletariat is afraid to enter one temple. This god is beauty, this temple—art."

8. Viktor B. Shklovskii, "Ullia, Ullia, Marsiane!" *Khod konia* (Berlin, 1923), p. 39. This article first appeared in *Iskusstvo kommuny* (March 30, 1919). The title is a reminder to Khlebnikov of the independent position he espoused before the October revolution. In a strident manifesto called "The Trumpet of the Martians," he had contemptuously denounced the philistines and declared that he would withdraw the Futurists from their society and declare them Martians, with H. G. Wells and Marinetti invited to their Duma as consultants. The agenda would include the subject "Ullia, Ullia, Marsiane." This manifesto has been reprinted in N. Brodskii, V. Lvov-Rogachevskii, *Literaturnye manifesty* (M., 1929), pp. 83-86.

9. Shklovskii, *Khod konia,* pp. 37-41. Professor Barooshian, in his otherwise excellent account of this period, should not have included Shklovsky in the list of artists and critics who aligned themselves with *Narkompros* (see Vahan D. Barooshian, "The Avant-Garde and the Russian Revolution," *Russian Literature Triquarterly,* 4 [Fall, 1972], p. 349. In *A Sentimental Journey,* Shklovsky refers to Belinsky as "the killer of Russian literature" and he expresses the wish to trample him with the legs of his writing desk.

10. *Ibid.*, pp. 12-17.

11. See Victor Erlich, *Russian Formalism* (3rd edition; The Hague, 1969 [1st ed., 1955]), p. 136. This book also downgrades Shklovsky's role as the founder of the movement and leaves the impression that the Moscow Linguistic Circle preceded *Opoyaz*—a misconception recently corrected in Ewa M. Thompson's book *Russian Formalism and Anglo-American New Criticism* (The Hague, 1971). This misconception results mainly from the fact that Professor Erlich never mentions in his text even the title of Shklovsky's booklet *Resurrection of the Word* (Petersburg, 1914). The title is simply listed in the bibliography, though nearly every treatment of Formalism has recognized that booklet as the cornerstone of the movement (Eikhenbaum, Medvedev, Markov, Lo Gatto, Ivan Vinogradov). Professor Erlich does mention *Resurrection of the Word* in his doctoral thesis, where he disagrees with those who consider it fundamental: "This seems to be something of an overstatement. While Shklovsky's critical debut undoubtedly anticipates some aspects of Formalist theory, especially the author's subsequent notion of making strange the object, it was, on the whole, too much of a hodgepodge to be construed as a coherent statement of a new school of criticism" (Columbia Dissertation, 1952, p. 133). *Resurrection of the Word* may or may not be a hodgepodge, but it nonetheless stimulated the formation of *Opoyaz* in 1914 and outlined, in inchoate form, the concerns to be pursued by the group during its initial stage. Shklovsky stressed the sound component of poetic language and he raised the question of what makes form perceptible. Even before its publication, the book was read to an assemblage at the Stray Dog cabaret in December, 1913, and it made an extremely favorable impression on the Futurists present (Benedikt Livshits, *Polutoroglazyi strelets* [L., 1933], pp. 200-201). After its publication, Shklovsky presented a copy to Baudouin de Courtenay, who introduced Shklovsky to his most brilliant students, Lev Yakubinsky and Evgeny Polivanov. They were intrigued by the notion of applying linguistic analysis to poetic language. A few months later, Brik, who shared Shklovsky's interest in Futurist poetry, became part of the group. Consequently, in its earliest formation, the nucleus of the movement consisted of "Futurists" like Shklovsky and Brik, united with the linguistics students of Baudouin de Courtenay. Eikhenbaum and Tynyanov joined the group much later; neither of them contributed to the first collections published by *Opoyaz* in 1916 and 1917.

12. D. G. B. Piper, *V. A. Kaverin: A Soviet Writer's Response to the Problem of Commitment* (Pittsburgh, 1970), p. 1.

13. Viktor B. Shklovskii, *Gamburgskii schet* (L., 1928), p. 107. See also his remarks in *Kak my pishem* (L., 1930), pp. 211-216.

14. See *A Sentimental Journey*, p. 117.

15. See Erlich, p. 131.

16. See Piper, pp. 50-52.

17. See my article "Shklovsky, Gorky and the Serapion Brothers," *The Slavic and East European Journal* (Spring, 1968), pp. 8-9.

18. See Edward J. Brown, *The Proletarian Episode in Russian*

Literature, 1928-1932 (New York, 1953), pp. 235-240, for an English translation of this resolution.

19. For an excellent discussion of these developments, see Herman Ermolaev, *Soviet Literary Theories 1917-1934: The Genesis of Socialist Realism* (Berkeley and Los Angeles, 1963), pp. 44-54. Professor Struve, who interpreted this party resolution as a Magna Carta in the 1950 edition of his book, recognizes in the new edition that Ermolaev's interpretation is compelling (see Gleb Struve, *Russian Literature under Lenin and Stalin* (Norman, 1971), p. 91. Professor Ermolaev did not use *Third Factory* in his analysis, but it supports his thesis.

20. See Ermolaev, p. 214.

21. Shklovskii, *Gamburgskii schet*, p. 109. *Hamburg Account* also contains Shklovsky's vehement protests against censorship in the film industry. He proclaims the importance of "artistic integrity" and says, *inter alia*, "It must be understood that in art there are no orders, that a too literal carrying out of orders has always been a form of sabotage" (p. 158).

22. Maxim Gorky, Letter to A. K. Voronsky, November 20, 1926 in *Letopis'zhizni i tvorchestva A. M. Gor'kogo*, ed. B. V. Mikhailovskii, L. I. Ponomarev and V. R. Shcherbina (4 vols.; M., 1958-1960), Vol. III, p. 486.

23. A. Lezhnev, *Sovremenniki* (M., 1927), pp. 133-138. This article first appeared under the title "Tri knigi" in *Pechat' i Revoliutsiia*, 8 (1926), pp. 80-86.

24. O. M. Beskin, "Kustarnaia masterskaia literaturnoi reaktsii," *Na literaturnom postu*, 7 (1927), pp. 18-20.

25. See V. V. Maiakovskii, "Vystuplenie na dispute 'LEF ili blef?',」" held on March 23, 1927, *Polnoe Sobranie Sochinenii* (13 vols.; M., 1955-1961), XII, 345-350.

26. Viktor B. Shklovskii, *Udachi i porazheniia Maksima Gor'kogo* (Tiflis, 1927), p. 62.

27. See A. V. Lunacharskii, "Formadzm v nauke ob iskusstve," *Pechat' i Revoliutsiia*, 5 (1924), p. 26. Shklovsky conducted a similar running debate with Trotsky during the twenties. In *Knight's Move*, Shklovsky had presented five propositions demonstrating the falsity of the Marxist conception of art. In his book *Literature and Revolution*, Trotsky refuted these propositions point by point and then concluded his chapter: "The Formalists show a fast-ripening religiosity. They are followers of St. John. They believe that 'In the beginning was the Word.' But we believe that in the beginning was the deed. The word followed, as its phonetic shadow." See L. Trotsky, *Literature and Revolution* (Ann Arbor, 1960), p. 183.

In his introduction to *Theory of Prose*, Shklovsky had the last word: "It is perfectly clear that language is influenced by social relations. . . .

All the same, the word is not a shadow.

The word is a thing."

28. I. M. Nusinov, "Zapozdalye otkrytiia, ili kak V. Shklovskomu nadoelo est' golymi formalistskimi rukami i obzavelsia samodel'noi marksistkoi lozhkoi," *Literatura i Marksizm*, 5 (1929), pp. 3-52. Nusinov

was arrested during the purge of Jewish intellectuals in the late 1940s and died in 1950.

29. See I. Grossman-Roshchin, "Bank obshchestvennogo doveriia ili bogadel'nia deklassirovannykh" in *S kem i pochemu my boremsia*, ed. L. L. Averbakh (M., 1930), pp. 166-174. This article first appeared in *Oktiabr'*, No. 6, 1929.

30. Shklovskii, *Gamburgskii schet*, p. 52.

31. Kaverin's book, *Skandalist, ili vechera na Vasil'evskom ostrove*, first appeared serially in the journal *Zvezda*, Nos. 2-7, 1928. It appeared in book form in 1929 and has been published several times since. All quotations are taken from the 1931 edition.

32. *Ibid.*, p. 349.

33. *Ibid.*, p. 459.

34. Veniamin Kaverin, "Poiski i resheniia," *Novyi mir*, 11 (November, 1954), pp. 187-88.

35. See Viktor B. Shklovskii, *O Maiakovskom* (M., 1940), pp. 208-214.

36. Boris Eikhenbaum, however, courageously defended his longtime friend. See his article, "O Viktore Shklovskom," in *Moi vremennik* (L., 1929), pp. 131-32.

37. G. Gukovskii, "Shklovskii kak istorik literatury," *Zvezda*, 1 (1930), pp. 191-216.

38. Erlich, p. 137.

39. Jules Romains, *Donogoo Tonka ou Les Miracles de la Science: Conte cinematographique* (Paris, 1920).

40. Shklovskii, "Pamiatnik," p. 1.

41. Erlich, p. 139.

42. M. Gelfand, "Deklaratsiia tsaria Midasa, ili cho, sluchilos' s Viktorom Shklovskim," *Literaturnaia gazeta*, 9 (March 3, 1930), p. 2. This article was also printed in *Pechat' i Revoliutsiia*, 2 (1930), pp. 8-15.

43. Viktor B. Shklovskii, "Sukhoplavtsy, ili uravnenie s odnim neizvestnym," *Literaturnaia gazeta*, 13 (March 31, 1930), p. 2. On the same page, Gelfand replied in a short article entitled "Otvet neponiatnomu."

44. It should be pointed out that there has been a tendency to accept Professor Erlich's interpretation of "Monument" without examining the original document. See, for example, the introduction to *Russian Formalist Criticism*, trans. Lee Lemon and Marion Reis (Lincoln, 1965), pp. IX-XVII. See also Ewa M. Thompson, *Russian Formalism and Anglo-American New Criticism* (The Hague and Paris, 1971), p. 33.

45. See "Usilit' bor' bu s formalizmom," *Literaturnaia gazeta*, 17 (April 11, 1933), p. 1. See the entry on Formalism, *Bol'shoe sovetskoe entsiklopediia* (M., 1926-1947), Vol. LXII, p. 441.

46. Viktor B. Shklovskii, "Iugo-zapad," *Literaturnaia gazeta*, 1 (January 5, 1933). Shklovsky was forced to print a retraction, which appeared as a letter to the editor in *Literaturnaia gazeta*, 20 (April 29, 1933).

Viktor Shklovsky

THIRD FACTORY

I CONTINUE

I speak in a voice grown hoarse from silence and feuilletons.
I'll begin with a piece that has been lying around for a long time.

The way you assemble a film by attaching to the beginning either a piece of exposed negative or a strip from another film.

I am attaching a piece of theoretical work. The way a soldier crossing a stream holds his rifle high.

It will be completely dry. Dry as a cough.

During the eighteenth century and at the beginning of the nineteenth, to tell an anecdote meant to relate an interesting fact about something.

For instance, to relate that the Krupp factory is currently building a diesel engine with 2,000 horsepower in one cylinder would have been, from the viewpoint of that time, an anecdote. An anecdotal story, from the viewpoint of that time, was also a story consisting of separate facts tenuously connected. There were even such things as philosophical anecdotes.

Wit—the unexpected denouement, for instance—had no place in the anecdote of that time. Now we describe an anecdote as a short novella with a denouement. From our viewpoint, to ask after hearing an anecdote, "But what happened next?" is an absurdity, but then that is the viewpoint of our time.

In the old days, one anecdotal fact was normally followed by another. In the old anecdote, one responded above all to the attractiveness of the fact, to the material, whereas in the modern anecdote we respond mainly to the structure.

This conflict—or, rather, the alternation—of perception from one aspect of a work to another—can be traced easily.

I have no desire to be witty.

I have no desire to construct a plot.

I am going to write about things and thoughts.

To compile quotations.

The time has changed course once again and the word "anecdote," once applied to a witty story, will soon be defined in terms of the various facts being printed in the this-and-that columns of the newspapers. Each separate moment of a play is becoming a separate, self-contained entity. Structure is usually missing. When it does creep into a piece of work, it is promptly killed; moreover, the crime goes unnoticed by the public. And the crime is pointless: the victim is already dead. The interest in the adventure novel which we are now witnessing does not contradict the thought just expressed. What we have in the adventure novel is a type of "stringing" in which there is no orientation toward the connecting thread.[1]

At the present time, we perceive memoirs as literature; we respond to them as something esthetic.

This is clearly not due to interest in the revolution, because people are avid to read even memoirs having absolutely nothing to do with the revolutionary epoch.

It goes without saying that plot-oriented prose still exists and will continue to exist, but it has been consigned to the attic.

FIRST FACTORY

ABOUT A RED ELEPHANT

"Red elephant, my son[2] would be lost without you. I'm letting you into my book ahead of the others to keep them in their place."

The red elephant is squeaking. All rubber toys are supposed to squeak; why else would the air come out?

And so, Brehm[3] notwithstanding, the red elephant is squeaking. And I, perched high in my nest above the Arbat,[4] am writing.

No bird could scale these heights without huffing and puffing. Here in my nest, I have learned not to be longwinded.

My son is laughing.

He started laughing the first time he saw a horse; he thought it was doing four legs and a long nose just for fun.

We are cranked out in various shapes, but we speak in one voice when pressure is applied.

"Red elephant, step aside. I want to see life seriously and to say something to it in a voice not filtered through a squeaker."

Here ends the feuilleton.

I WRITE ABOUT HOW OBJECTIVE REALITY DETERMINES CONSCIOUSNESS, WHILE THE CONSCIENCE REMAINS IN DISARRAY

All his life, Mark Twain wrote double letters: one he sent and the other he wrote for himself—and there he wrote what he thought.

Pushkin, too, wrote rough drafts of his letters.

The last days of autumn. They echo with the sound of the leaves withering in the lanes called Skatertny, Chashnikovy, Khlebny. (It sounds like someone sweeping out rejected

7

manuscripts). Someone is playing a violin, too. I have no right to keep quiet about that.

Caught in the green arc of the streetlamps, the streets march in formation beside me.

I sing plaintively as I go:

> No, you surely are not dear to me
> Those who care are not like that.[5]

Editorial offices have plywood partitions. Thoughts that are hide-bound. After those sessions, it was always a relief to get outside.

I am leaking like a frayed rubber hose. The book will be called

THIRD FACTORY

First of all, I have a job at the third factory of Goskino.[6]

Second of all, the name isn't hard to explain. The first factory was my family and school. The second was *Opoyaz*.

And the third—is processing me at this very moment.

Do we really know how a man ought to be processed?

Maybe it's all right to make him stand in line for things. Maybe it's all right for him to work outside his specialty.

That's not the elephant squeaking—that is my voice.

The time cannot be mistaken; the time cannot have wronged me.

It's wrong to say: "The whole squad is out of step except for one ensign." I want to speak with my time, to understand its voice. Right now, for example, it's hard for me to write, because the normal length for an article will soon be reached.

But chance is crucial to art. The dimensions of a book have always been dictated to an author.

The marketplace gave a writer his voice.

A work of literature lives on material. *Don Quixote* and *The Minor*[7] owe their existence to unfreedom.

It is impossible to exclude certain material; necessity creates works of literature. I need the freedom to work from my own plans; freedom is needed if the material is to be bared. I don't want to be told that I have to make bentwood chairs out of rocks. At this moment, I need time and a reader. I want to write about unfreedom, about the royalties paid by Smirdin,[8] about the influence of journals on literature, about the third factory— life. We *(Opoyaz)* are not cowards and we do not bend before wind pressure. We love the wind of the revolution. Air moving a hundred kilometers an hour exerts pressure. When a car slows down to seventy-five kph, the pressure drops. That is unbearable. Nature abhors a vacuum. Full speed ahead.

And let me cultivate my own garden. It's wrong for everyone to sow wheat. I am unable to squeak like the elephant.

It's wrong to coddle art. We have nothing in common with the gold-tipped Abram Efros.[9]

That is just about all.

THE CHILDHOOD OF A WRITER WHO EVENTUALLY LEARNED TO BE SUCCINCT

During the night, I had the usual dream: I was on the lookout for an enemy in the room, and I was crying.

Morning began.

I had a gray blouse (I've never liked that word) with an elastic band around the bottom. My summer cap also had an elastic band. I chewed the elastic. Even my socks had elastic bands—red ones.

Our family had neither bicycles nor dogs. Once we kept some chicks that were late in hatching next to the stove. They had a bad case of rickets, which I treated with strips of paper.

Much later, I had a finch that was kept in a wooden cage. The finch sang his song at six A.M.; I, unfortunately, woke up at eight. Eventually, a rat got him.

I'm an old man now. When I was a boy, people still fell under streetcars that were drawn by horses—sometimes one, sometimes two.

I saw the coming of electricity. It was still crawling on all fours and burning with a yellow light. I saw the coming of the telephone.

I saw students being beaten. The workers lived so far away that on our street, Nadezhenskaya, you hardly ever heard about them. Their part of town was reached by one of those horse-drawn streetcars.

I remember the Boer War and a hectographic picture: a Boer spanking an Englishman. I remember the arrival of the French in Petersburg,[10] the beginning of the twentieth century, the ice breaking up on the Neva.

My grandfather was a gardener at the Smolny Institute. A big, gray-haired German.[11] He had in his room a blue, glass sugarbowl and some things covered with dark cotton. Behind his house curved the Neva and I saw something bright and small.

I don't remember what.

I didn't like having my buttons buttoned and unbuttoned.

I learned to read from blocks without pictures. Rough wood showed on the corners of each block. I remember the block with the letter "A." I would recognize it even now. I remember the feel of a green metal pail on the teeth. The feel of toys in general. Of disappointment.

We went for walks in the small square by the church of Kozma and Demian. We called it "Kozma and Simian." On the other side of the wall bounding the square was a storehouse. We thought monkeys lived there. . . . The storehouse had a chimney. The grownups would lose their tempers.

We were wild and unruly. Grownups failed to get through

to us. They rarely do get through. I remember the jingle:

> Viktoor, cheapest doctoor
> Ever seen.
> Smears your nose
> With kerosene.

There was measles, too. Some were given milk kissel, others bilberry. All four of us were sick at the same time.

Basseinaya Street was still paved with wood. At that time, people in the city were still delighted when orchards were cut down. We were true city dwellers.

There was also the journal *Niva*,[12] bound in red and gold. There were pictures in it: trolleycar races. The bicycle had already been invented and people were as proud of them as they are now of the principle of relativity.

At the rim of the city, beyond the wind-swept Neva, was Vasily Island, and there, an hour and a half from our place, stood the brown house where Uncle Anatoly lived. He had a telephone and at Eastertime we were served blue raisins and eggs that were gilded but inedible.

On the dressing table of his diminutive wife stood a triptych mirror and a pink piggy bank. For me, that piggy bank marked the rim of the world.

THE DACHA

Our apartment slowly filled with furniture; my parents were getting rich. They bought heavy silver spoons. A cabinet with glass panes. Bronze candelabra, too, and they upholstered the furniture with red plush. That summer, everyone was buying a dacha.

Papa bought a dacha at the seashore. It was bought on credit. The land was sandy and swampy, with sedge, sand and juniper in abundance. We cut the juniper down ourselves, with a dull ax. Papa thought that juniper was strewn about at funerals. What they strew about at funerals is pine.

The bark of the juniper is dry and blue, but the wood is as solid as bone. It makes good handles for tools.

Juniper and pine grew in patches along the sea. These patches served as a hedge. We put up a gate and printed a sign. In letters blue and gold:

Dacha Tranquility.

Then hard times began.

Fewer lightbulbs in our rooms.

No more new clothes. Mama's hair turned silver. The same color it is today.

We puttered around the dacha. Papa pawned his fur coat and worked. We planted pines in the sand along the hedge. They are now three times my height. The years have gone by.

Mama made the rounds of the creditors to persuade them to wait. The furniture was sold at auction. There were very many tears.

Being the last child in the family, I ripened like grain sown out of season. We lived in the country, in our dacha. Huge windows, snow outside the windows, snow on the ice all the way to Kronstadt. Ice is jagged on the sea, like asphalt broken to make street repairs.

A MULTIFARIOUS GYMNASIUM

Cold Petersburg on a gray morning. The gymnasium.

I was a bad student and I attended bad schools. At first my parents wanted to put me in a good school, into the Third Modern.[13] I took an exam there.

12

Behind the glass doors loomed silent classrooms. Pupils in their places, like rows of coats on hangers. Empty corridors, empty stairways, a reception room with a tile floor done in big checks.

The corridors had parquet floors, trod by a little old man in a service uniform—Richter, the headmaster.

It was a seven-year school.

I got no farther than the tile floor: spelling was my downfall.

Then I entered a private modern school—Boginsky's. Looking down from there, I could see, on Znamenskaya Square, a vacant lot overgrown with grass; the view included a boarded-up outhouse.

The Alexander monument stands there now.

I was taken out of that school because it was very expensive.

I was excluded from gymnasium to gymnasium. As a result, my gray coat had to be dyed black and embellished with a cat-fur collar.

That is how THE overcoat was made.[14]

I started preparing for entrance exams. I read a lot, I stopped smoking. My hair was already thin, but the curls were still intact.

The frenzied efforts of my parents to save the dacha were to no avail. They were ineffectual people. The mortgage was foreclosed; the dacha was sold.

Then things took a turn for the better. Once again we bought candelabra and silver, though a lighter variety than before.

I failed the entrance exams for the cadet corps.

It was decided to send me to a gymnasium. To graduate from a gymnasium required a minimum of three years.

The gymnasium was fully accredited and hopeless. It was overrun with rejects from other schools. The principal of the gymnasium was Doctor Sh., a man from Arkhangelsk, blond and unprepossessing, virtually lacking eyes and face. He wore a black frock coat, rumpled and generously daubed with lint. . . .

The red elephant is speaking without much enthusiasm. He wants to talk about love.

But love, as Larisa Reisner[15] said to me, is a play with short acts and long intermissions. One must know how to behave during the intermissions. . . .

. . . .
. . . .

As for the doctor in question, I am chewing him absent-mindedly, like hay.

He had been a student of Pavlov,[16] and a very talented student at that.

I stay afloat, dog paddling—maybe my struggles will generate some whipped cream.

Next door to the doctor lived a man of genius. He had started the gymnasium to make some money. His students were the worst possible, while he was a combination of science and duplicity. He looked at us evasively, like a shopkeeper peddling worthless goods, and he looked at us piercingly, like a physiologist.

He was very Russian.

Nikolai Petrovich had his own pedagogical theories.

"Up to the age of five," he would say, "a child is taught nothing, but he learns more than he does the rest of his life."

All things considered, a bad school is good schooling. If the students break the pewter inkwells, you just give them glass ones—they're not so much fun to break.

On the whole, nothing fazed Nikolai Petrovich—things went a little better or a little worse. He would wander through the gymnasium losing his temper and putting his hands in the urinals to fish out cigarette butts.

He was as bored as an usher during the performance or a spectator during intermission.

One thing I want to say about this man—he loved like an usher.

Periodically, the Ministry of Education sent around district inspectors.

The class froze, well aware of its ignorance. The truth was, we knew nothing at all. Not even the decimals.

The district inspector would first of all check under the desks to see if we were wearing high boots. Then he would check the tops of the desks. Then he would sit down beside some student, take his notebooks and flip through them.

He generally shook out a pony or two for Horace.

Then he headed for the toilet to check for cigarette butts in the urinals.

The teachers varied; the turnover was rapid. These were Soviet civil servants, fifteen years ago.

GRADUATION TIME

Science, pale and gaunt, clung to the pages of our books and refused to come out.

We drank a little as we sat in the gray classrooms (ashberry brandy—the bottles were tossed behind the stove). We played Twenty-One under the desks. We read almost nothing. But I was already writing prose and writing about prose theory. We never gave a thought to the phenomenon known as community spirit. Had we wanted to change our ways, we would have no doubt made amends by preparing for our Latin classes.

We did have a good Latinist—the venerable principal from Arkhangelsk, also from Kursk, Astrakhan and Kitais. He had been driven from gymnasium to gymnasium, always on the move, but he took with him the most desperate students, knowing that they had to finish somewhere.

In Vologda, where he came from originally, he was popular. All the boats on the Volga skirted his favorite fishing hole.

He taught me about *ut consecutivum*.

Cars drove past the gymnasium on cobblestones that resembled the keyboard of a grand piano; the streetcar wires hummed like a tuning fork. On the other side of the Neva, you could make out the black fretwork of the Summer Garden against a green net. The Summer Garden.

That garden was beginning to turn green. Spring was creeping under coats and over bosoms with its insistent breeze.

We were seated in a big auditorium—a good two yards apart. Exams were being given.

We used cribs, exchanged information and practically rapped out messages to each other.

Our teachers wandered down the aisles on their less-than-vigilant patrols. I wrote sixteen compositions for that exam.

One of our classmates dozed off during this tense period. His neighbor woke him up.

"Vaska, don't sleep—write!"

"The writing will get done," he answered grandly, dozing off again.

It was this handsome, blue-eyed lad who had read Latin verses from a book held by the district inspector.

So much for the art of living topsy-turvy.

Where are you, friends!

Where are you, Klimovetsky? Where is Enisevsky? Killed, they say, during the defense of Tsaritsyn.

Where is Tarasov? I know about Brook.

Surovtsev is an aviator. If we should meet now, each of us would be dismayed at how the other has aged. There would be no point in such a meeting.

All this came to pass across from the lycée on Kamennoostrovsky Prospekt. . . .

THE DEBT I OWE MY TEACHER

I did best of all on the religion exam. By chance, I knew the history of the church from courses at the university. Even now, my spelling leaves something to be desired. That is why I went to my teacher's house after the Russian exam. This old man had been an assistant professor and had studied under Potebnya[17] at one time; then he had exchanged scholarship for civil service, and the civil service had not panned out.

He had missed his chance.

It was pitch dark when I called on this man. I rang the bell. He opened the door for me himself. Decked out in a service uniform and probably wearing a decoration around his neck.

"So you've come. Your work is lying on my desk. Did you bring any ink from the gymnasium?"

"No."

"Well, I've gotten some ready myself."

So, under the cover of night, on Gulyarnaya Street, I furtively corrected my mistakes.

"All right, Shklovsky," my teacher said, "just dedicate your master's thesis to me."

I have no master's thesis at the moment; I wrote none.

But to you, old teacher, I hereby dedicate this spot in a work bearing no resemblance to a master's thesis.

You took pity on my spelling.

I WRITE ABOUT KISSES

She loved me and didn't make me suffer. We kissed each other, though we hardly knew how.

And once we were exchanging kisses toward morning when something red suddenly banged at the window and the woman in question started screaming. It was the tsar's name-day and the wind had shoved a flag into our window; it chose the bottom half.

The sun was rising.

In the morning, the streets were deserted, the bridges raised and the sun rising behind the crosses on the right bank of the Neva.

17

I slept little and occasionally fainted. To love a woman and the hat she wears, to remember her for twelve or fifteen years—is nice.

MORE ABOUT THE FIRST FACTORY

What I remember best of all about the university is the corridor. Standing in that vast hall, a man seemed small. The corridor was warm and bright. Unfortunately, the end of it did not overlook the Neva. A piece had been cut off to make an office for the vice-rector.

In the corridor were notes, hanging on plywood boards. Going off the corridor were dark passageways, leading to lecture rooms.

The university offices and museums—I'm speaking about the Department of Philology—were small. To find the university in the university was very hard. It was hard to figure out where the learning was going on: in the lecture room with the bad portraits of scholars on the walls, in the warm corridor or in the professors' apartments?

The university did teach us a thing or two about community spirit: the lines we stood in to register were the most organized in the world. I believe standing in line originated at the university and spread from there throughout Mother Russia. Decked out in a special costume—heavy, diagonal, green pants and a green frock coat with gold buttons—I entered the university.

That frock coat had already graduated from the university once; it had danced a lot on my older brother. My brother danced in such a way that the watch in his pocket rusted, but the frock coat underwent no change.

I eventually sold it in 1919 at the Maltsevoi Market, across from the red building of the Evangelical Hospital.

I hope it is now graduating from a workers' school.[18]

I attended and listened.

But the university wasn't working in my specialty. Nothing was being done about prose theory, though I was already working on it.

If before my death I manage to tear myself away for a minute to do what I do best, if I write the history of the Russian journal as a literary form, if I manage to analyze how *The Arabian Nights* is made, and can once again ply my trade, then perhaps there will be talk of putting my portrait in the university building.

Hang my portrait in the university corridor, friends. Tear down the vice-rector's study, establish a window on the Neva and sail past me on your bicycles.

SECOND FACTORY

A woman has love and love compels
her to seek lovers.
Stay put, phrase, and keep an eye
on things while I go get some other words.

THE SUMMER AFTER GYMNASIUM

I spent the summer in Nyslott, near Olaf Castle[19]—the place
where water runs from the Northern Saimaa into the Southern.
The current never freezes, never glazes with ice. In wintertime
the channel steams like a winded horse. From the mountains
loom other mountains.

One mountain looks like pieces of sugar tossed on a saucer
for tea. The others look like something or other, too. Water
collects between the mountains as in ruts. In fact, the whole
region is like a heavily traveled dirt road after a downpour.

At night, the frequently flickering lights that mark the
channel hiss.

A flickering light is visible from a greater distance than a
steady light. The channel ran around the castle; our rowboat
was jostled and knocked about. Just for a lark, my brother and I
had decided to row around the castle. The current was especially strong under a stone bridge, where the waves created a
bottleneck.

On the bridge stood a policeman, fishing. Next to him was
a stall that sold seltzer water and wild strawberries in little
boxes made of birchbark.

Many years later I landed in Finland once again.[20]

The dachas were tipped over, like bins in a plundered store.

Everything was more spacious—the forests had been cut
down.

During the civil war,[21] people killed each other here.
Everyone fought. During battle, husbands killed wives, lovers
killed husbands. Then the body was dumped outside, in the
line of fire, where bullets were flying.

When the Whites killed a Red, they tore out his tongue—

via the throat. The Reds killed in less elaborate ways.

Now those chopped-down forests are quiet. Finland is pretending not to notice the long Russian border. The way a bad actor wants the curtain to sever him from the audience. His legs quake. But the curtain is nonexistent. The auditorium looms like a gulf. And standing in front of that gulf at Nyslott was a policeman, fishing off the bridge.

That summer I watched the flickering lights of Nyslott.

The girl whose shoes, wide-brimmed hat, dark face and clinging dress I remember after fifteen years didn't write to me then.

She had gone to the Carpathians and then another four hundred kilometers through the mountains on foot. There she found sand, pine trees and spruce. Eventually our prisoners built a road.

THE VOICE OF A SEMIPROCESSED COMMODITY

We are flax in the field.

We lie in our flat patches. We are acted upon by the sun and bacteria—what are they called anyway?

And to my right is a shelf of Tolstoy.

One of his words has been lying in this field with me for ten years. I'll check the passage.

> I remember walking down the street once in Moscow and seeing a man step outside ahead of me and peer at the stones in the sidewalk; then he selected one stone, crouched over it and began (or so it seemed to me) to scrape or rub with singular strain and effort.
>
> What is he doing to that sidewalk? I thought. When I got right up to him, I saw what this man

was doing. It was a young man from the butcher shop: he was sharpening his knife on a stone in the sidewalk. He had no thought for the stones at all, though he was scrutinizing them; still less was he thinking about them while performing his task—he was sharpening his knife. He had to sharpen his knife in order to cut meat; I had thought he was doing something to the stones in the sidewalk. In exactly the same way, man appears to be busy with commerce, treaties, wars, the arts, the sciences when one thing matters to him and that one thing is all that he does: he is clarifying for himself the moral laws by which he lives. . . .[22]

I have nothing against the late Tolstoy. His art is what matters—and that's all.

For example. It doesn't matter whether we lie in the field, whether we suffer or rejoice. What matters is the sharpening of the knife, i.e. art.

And the stones on which we are being sharpened lie in a different realm; they have been laid a different way; we need them, but they run a different way.

And what if I love the stone, the wind—what if today I have no need for the knife?

Flax does not cry out in the brake. What I need today is not a book and movement forward: I need a destiny, and grief as heavy as red corals.

An oyster draws the valves of its shell together with a supreme effort. Having drawn them shut, it stops functioning. Its muscles no longer radiate heat, but they do hold the valves shut.

Prose and poetry are being held shut in such a death grip. Muscles warm and living could never exert the necessary force.

Thirty-three-year-old shell, I am sick today. I know how heavy is the force that keeps the valves together. That should not be.

What I need today is not a book. Life is passing by, taking me along as a guide for the day. Life, I want to open the valves and talk to you.

Look me in the eye, life.

I lie in my field; no dacha was ever so fine.

I DOG PADDLE

The students in the dark auditorium were listening to a lecture by Baudouin de Courtenay, a philologist who changed much in that science, but who proved unable to write a book. The book was written later—by Meillet.[23]

During his first year in the Department of Philology, a budding philologist had to pass an exam in Greek—something on the order of translating a book of Xenophon.

I failed the exam.

Then the Futurists appeared on the scene.

But before telling why I so gladly stuck yellow artificial flowers into the cuff of my frock coat, I'll tell what it was like to be a sculptor.

I may as well admit that the walls of our house were covered with very bad pictures; only the strange, extravagant and desperate taste of my father, who was putting up a dacha with no plan (while the money lasted), saved our abode from being a complete disaster.

I read a lot, but was unfamiliar with the Symbolists.

I did see the journal *Vesy* occasionally and I was embarrassed by the cover of *Apollon*, which showed a man whose nakedness was covered only by the letters "Let Us Be Like the Sun."[24]

The letters were translucent.

SHERWOOD

As a neophyte sculptor, I went to Ilya Ginzburg.[25]

In that way, I found out about academic corridors before encountering those at the university.

Behind one of the doors lining one of those corridors with passageways going off in four directions, I found Ilya Ginzburg.

There in his studio, behind an iron grating, a small monkey was chattering—with a strong Jewish accent.

Ilya Ginzburg was a very short man and he had a weak hand.

He praised my sculpture, but I soon moved to Kazan Street, where Sherwood[26] had his studio. In that studio, filled with dry heat and the smell of wet clay, Sherwood was bald and strict.

What I had instead of talent was a quiet frenzy which could not be accommodated.

I attacked the clay furiously and was easily pleased.

Sherwood explained the meaning of form to me and showed me that sculpting had nothing to do with capturing an expression. He taught me how to sculpt the napes of necks and to seek out general form.

During the famine, Sherwood lived off the money he made by breeding his goat.

I never became a sculptor, but I learned a lot.

Sculpting with me was a feeble man with too small a heart. He sculpted well and then became an architect. He ought to be building important buildings, but he lacks the ability to navigate a meatgrinder, so we behold in him great talent badly accommodated in a feeble body. His name is Rakuzin.

He is undaunted by life.

Sherwood and wet clay taught me to understand art correctly.

SCIENCE AND DEMOCRACY

Then the Futurists appeared on the scene.

David Burlyuk with his raised eyebrow, Kruchyonykh, Nikolai Burlyuk, also in a frock coat, and Vladimir Mayakovsky, still wearing his black velvet jacket, lectured on the Futurists. They were becoming fashionable.[27]

The stairway of literary tendencies leads to a false door. That particular stairway exists while you are climbing it.[28]

Kruchyonykh has been publishing himself for many years now. David Burlyuk is in America.

At that time, Mayakovsky had a black top hat and a voice—a bass that issued from a black mouth.

The Futurists were being persecuted. Several times pacts were made to write nothing about them.

But we proved stronger than the Azov-Don Bank.

Just don't try to walk through a false door.

The Futurists started out with new images and "transrational" language. It was as though an avalanche had bared strata never seen before and out from under the clay, driving away the dogs, had crawled a living mammoth.

Mayakovsky, Kruchyonykh and Chukovsky were performing for some women med students once. Chukovsky was contrasting the Futurists to science and democracy in general.

One of the Futurists said something disrespectful about Korolenko.[29]

A screech went up. Mayakovsky cut through the crowd like a hot iron through snow. Kruchyonykh defended himself with his galoshes. Science and democracy were pinching him—they loved Korolenko.

DOCTOR NIKOLAI IVANOVICH KULBIN[30]

He was tall and his small, round head was bald. A khaki tunic. He painted on aluminum. What he valued in art was chance. A dilettante, he believed that sun spots had made the revolution possible, that Evreinov[31] was a genius and that it pays to tell a man he's a genius, because a man will walk a tightrope if he believes he can.

He loved to kiss women's hands for them. He was unable to write articles, but he was continually using colored pencils to make posters with triangular aphorisms about how rocks fall to earth because they love it.

Just before he died, he made another poster:

My sole . . . consolation = solitude.

Before that, he had hung the walls of his room with paintings done on aluminum and hand-painted plates; he also painted the columns of his buffet blue.

The painted buffet underwent no change.

The doctor's life was not regulated by sun spots. Women's hands flashed by like piano keys.

The solitude around the painted buffet was replaced by the revolution. The sun had led him to expect it.

Kulbin died happy on the third day after his expectation was realized. He liked me and considered me his successor. He had been paying me three rubles a day to influence his son and make him turn out like me. He taught me what foods to eat.

Kulbin's son eventually served in the militia, fought against bandits, made soap out of horsemeat and joined the Komsomol.

The family had a hard time selling their grand piano; what they are living on now, I have no idea.

Kulbin used to say that the Acmeists had a sluggish circulatory system. He promised that I would be spared anemia, but to watch out for sclerosis.

He ordered me to sleep ten hours a day.

Nikolai Ivanovich, you had a good death. I wonder—what road would you have taken?

Stairways lead to false doors. Now that the volcanoes have stopped erupting, the soup has come to a boil and is being poured into various bowls.

You promised me genius.

That's a present I won't return.

I'll try once more to walk the tightrope.

I am getting a lot of sleep.

Sergei Gorodetsky, whom you liked, is not writing at all. He is living in the building where Ksenya Godunov was strangled long ago and where, later on, Pugachyov was held before his execution.

A solid building. Still later, Novikov printed books there.[32] Now it's an apartment building.

When Vasilisk Gnedov was fighting by the Nikita Gate, a building there was demolished by cannon fire.

Stunned, Gnedov lapsed into poetry.[33]

Pronin[34] runs around without aging—his wrinkles are all on the palms of his hands.

Blok is dead. Belenson[35] is alive.

Kornei Ivanovich Chukovsky is already a grandfather; his soul still harbors a dusty ventilator.

"Beware above all," said Kulbin, "gonorrhea. Gonorrhea takes something out of a man."

BAUDOUIN DE COURTENAY, BLOK, YAKUBINSKY

Futurism and sculpture made it possible to learn a lot. At that time, I saw art as an autonomous system. That conception of art stayed with me throughout the entire second factory. Armed with a thirty-two-page booklet set in pica (*Resurrection of the Word*),[36] I presented myself to Baudouin de Courtenay.[37]

A great, cantankerous old man.

I found myself in a professorial apartment full of bookshelves.

30

Those shelves lined the walls and extended into the middle of the room. The shelves were lined with books. A whole nation of books.

Later, during the Great Revolution, those shelves were burned to ashes, but the books, books of professors, were scattered all over the world.

Now they are forming new companies.

Besides books, the room contained deteriorating furniture.

I sat down on a chair set at an angle to the desk.

Chairs are placed in that position so that students can sit there and quiver. I quivered.

Baudouin is the king of Jerusalem, as he wrote once on his assistant professor's card in Kazan. Baudouin, or Bolduin, actually is the descendant of the first king of Jerusalem.

He heard me out and introduced me to Lev Yakubinsky.[38]

Writing books is hard, Lev Petrovich! It's hard to know how to write—or what.

Eskimoes tie themselves together with a strap when they sit over the airhole made by a seal in the ice.

The cold is fierce and hard to bear.

A bit more about Baudouin. He presided at a meeting and at the end started talking about science and democracy, but he didn't pinch.[39]

I became Yakubinsky's friend. He taught me a lot. This Yakubinsky has a timid step—like that of a compass afraid to bend its regulated legs.

I have made a lot of mistakes, Lev Petrovich, and I am still making them hand over fist. But then, flowers are unreliable, as opposed to botany.

I spent the second factory thinking—or, to put this in terms of an object being processed—undergoing the thought of freedom.

What concerns me now are the limits of freedom, the deformations of the material.

I want to change. I fear negative unfreedom. The denial of what others are doing partakes of them.

31

THERE WAS NO ROOM FOR A CANNON SHOT IN THE VALLEY OF THE VISTULA

War came along one day and stitched upon my shoulders the epaulets of a volunteer. War stood on the corner of Sadovaya and Inzhenernaya Streets and spoke to me in Blok's voice.

"In time of war, no one should think of himself."

Then he said to me: "Unfortunately, the majority of mankind consists of right-wing SR's."[40]

The walls of the city were plastered with war.

My brother was drafted. He lay in a khaki puptent, while Mama looked for him, crying out:

"Kolya, Kolya!"

When she had gone, the soldier next to him raised himself on one elbow and said:

"I feel sorry for you, Kolya."

WAR

The war was still young. The opposing sides converged on the battlefield. The soldiers were still young. Seeing each other face to face like that, they hated to use their bayonets. So they beat each other on the head with rifle butts. A soldier's pity.

A blow from a rifle butt splits the skull.

Our policemen were on duty in Galicia.[41]

During drinking bouts, prostitutes argued with our officers on the theme of Austria—whether it would revive. Those arguing never noticed that they were strangely dressed.

In Maupassant, this sort of thing is called "Fifi."[42] Our rendition came out dustier somehow—bound in dusty leather.

The war chewed me carelessly; I dribbled from its mouth like the hay being chewed by an overfed horse.

I returned to Petersburg and became an instructor in an armored division. Before that, I worked in a war plant.

I kept getting carbon-monoxide poisoning in the garage. I spat yellow spit. I lay on a slippery concrete floor, washing, fixing, cleaning.

The war was old by then. The morning and evening papers were interchangeable.

7 ZHUKOVSKY STREET

Foliage seems thickest of all by a city streetlamp, where you feel sorry for it: it belongs elsewhere.

Love probably doesn't exist. It is not a thing, but a landscape, consisting of a series of objects unconnected to each other, but seen as a whole.

But literature too is almost accidental. The writer fixes a mutation.

Just as we fix love.

But in one respect, love never varies. Like a shadow, it always extends its left hand to my right.

Pay attention to me, landscape. Extend your right hand to my right.

Someone telephoned me once and asked me to drop in on the volunteer Brik.

There was someone by that name in our squad. Everyone knew him: during a trial run, he had cracked up three cars. . . .

I went to the address—Zhukovsky Street, with a street-lamp in the middle. Asphalt. A high building. Number 7. Apartment 42.

The door opened. It was no door, but the cover of a book. I opened the book called *The Life Story of Osip and Lili Brik.*[43]

In the chapters of that book, my name occurs with some frequency.

I glance through it carelessly, like letters that you are still afraid to read.

On the first page was Brik. Not the one I knew, but another one. On the walls hung samplers from Turkestan. On the piano was an automobile made of cards, one cubic meter in size.

It goes without saying that people do not live for the purpose of having books written about them. But all the same, I like productive labor. I want people to do something.

O. M. B.

What is Osip Brik doing?

Osip Maksimovich Brik is now very much in evidence. Brik is a man chronically present and chronically evasive.

When I first met him, he was busy evading his military obligation.

His method was ingenious.

Brik was serving in a certain unit that was full of Jews. It was decided to send them, under escort, off to the infantry.

If Brik had balked, if he had spewed blood before the very eyes of the high command, he would have still been sent.

Each soldier got a piece of paper; the piece of paper said:

"ASSIGNMENT: Soldier such-and-such is hereby attached to the infantry."

Brik, armed with his piece of paper, proceeded to the station with the others.

At the station, however, he detached himself from his unit. He waited until the train left, turned down the collar of his overcoat, and presented himself to the commanding officer as if nothing had happened. He was now a "special case."

Wars are unable to cope with "special cases."

The commandant sent Brik to the transit barracks between Zagorodny Prospekt and the Fontanka.

Brik, like any soldier, was expendable.

And since he made no fuss and no attempt to clarify his situation, he remained in the transit barracks for a long time.

He treated the right people to dinner and they let him go home.

In Russia there were either eight million or twelve million soldiers.

Exactly how many were there? No one knew and no one will ever know.

I was told about this discrepancy of four million by Verkhovsky[44] when he was a minister.

Brik went to the barracks for a while, then stopped going.

He stayed home. For two years.

Dozens of people visited him and he published books, but his whereabouts remained unknown to the military.

A situation like this is very difficult; it requires a certain lack of enthusiasm for the government, a freedom from its will.

All this gets into the art of not filling out questionnaires.

Brik had to avoid only one thing—moving from apartment to apartment. He had to sit tight.

But he could have added three stories to the building he lived in and gone unnoticed.

For the time being, though, he confined himself to building a huge theater and an automobile made of cards on the piano.

Construction projects delighted Lili Brik.

Mayakovsky made frequent visits.

Mayakovsky—flax of the highest quality—won his first recognition at their place.

At that time, the newspapers were still stomping on him, while the humor magazines doused him with boiling water, drenched and pummeled him with abuse.

If you take into consideration the strength of the fiber, Mayakovsky leads the right kind of life.

He treats life like a motorcycle: when it conks out in the middle of the street, he patches it up without paying any attention to the curiosity seekers that gather around.

BRIK REMAINED IN ABSENTIA

All of us expected a catastrophe to engulf him at any moment.

Meanwhile, Brik took part in our work. He wrote a study of repetitions.[45]

Outwardly, his study demonstrates that a poem is riddled with sound patterns.

Rhyme is only a rim repetition.

Inwardly, his study shows that a poem is not a series of separate items, but a unified structure.

Brik mastered philological material with no difficulty whatsoever.

He was already beginning his major work—on rhythm.[46]

This study puts forward a new conception of rhythm; it restricts the meaning of that word, which had grown vague and meaningless in careless hands.

That study is still unfinished after seven years.

The chapter on Greek metrics was almost complete. Several thousand examples had been collected for the core of the article—a study of rhythmic-syntactic figures.

The chapter on the cesura was complete.

Two reports were given.

Brik demonstrated that a poem is not an organization of syllables, but an organization of words and sentences.

The study is still not done. Pieces of it went to Jakobson. Tynyanov[47] has some of it.

And Tomashevsky[48] has already retreated from the beachhead established by that article.

That is a big loss for the second factory.

Why isn't Brik writing?

He has no impulse toward achievement. He feels no urge to cut, so he refuses to sharpen the knife.

He is chronically evasive and chronically absent.

There is no achievement in his love. And all because of a cautious life.

You could cut off Brik's legs and he would promptly argue the advantages of being legless.

Brik, I've worked incorrectly all of my life, but I have worked. Now I'm at fault. I'm working little.

No meatgrinder can chop me up.

Every year on a certain day, the Jews stand at the table with staff in hand—signifying their readiness to strike out for new territory if the need arises.[49]

Never mind the Jews.

Let's strike out for new territory.

That will be easier with legs. Making mistakes is better than standing pat.

You, Brik, want to burn any cargo you can't take along.

You are repudiating art. You say it's finished. But it has only changed.

I'm writing a book. And meanwhile I'm working at Goskino.

A lot of things have changed. Snow has fallen.

The snow has lingered too long, like a woman beside her lover. Winter moved in on us with a suitcase.

My son, though still too young for school, has learned to walk and run and to say words like "Let's go" and "Give me."

He won't start school for four years.

"Brik, where's your book?" Larisa Reisner once asked you.

Brik, life has to be taken seriously.

Even a samovar refuses to boil without a draft. These are the doldrums, Brik.[50]

The earthquake is over. The lid has been removed, the soup has come to a boil, the spoons have been distributed. "Help yourselves," they say.

We have the right to refuse the spoons.

We are, after all, the "ideological superstructure."

The connection between us and the soup is complicated and non-functional.

We need a book—and you, Brik.

Or have you been frittered away with cups of tea?

Squandered in telephone conversations?
Depleted in small victories?

EVENINGS AT THE BRIKS

People were changing. That was probably advisable.

Vegetables, for example, are sometimes cooked in soup and then discarded.

It is essential, though, to understand what happens in that process. Otherwise, you can get the story wrong and mistake noise for work.

Noise is work for an orchestra, but not for the Putilov plant.

On the whole, we probably were vegetables.

But not according to the reading from our meridian.

And I—gazing at the samplers from Turkestan, stuffing the silk pillows behind the couch, smudging the upholstery with my leather pants, devouring everything on the table—I was cooked along with the others at the Briks.

On the table were these memorable items: 1) figs, 2) a big chunk of cheese, 3) liver pâté.

One issue of *Vzyal*[51] had been published.

Studies on the Theory of Poetic Language[52] had been published. What is important about the formal method?

Not the fact that the separate parts of a work can be given various labels.

The important thing is that we approached art systematically. We spoke about art as such. We refused to view it as a reflection. We located the distinctive features of the genus. We began defining the basic tendencies of form. We understood that, in fact, you can distill from works of literature the homogeneous laws that determine their shape.

In short, science is possible.

We had to start with sounds in order to divorce ourselves

from traditional material.

But even here we encountered false analogies.

There had been much discussion of onomatopoeia. Bely had discussed it.[53] Endlessly.

Our first collection included studies by Grammont and Nyrop which demonstrated the absence of a direct connection between the sound and the emotive components.[54]

We studied the sound component not from an emotive, but from a technical standpoint.

Vegetables of all kinds went into that soup.

TO ROMAN JAKOBSON, TRANSLATOR IN RESIDENCE FOR THE SOVIET EMBASSY IN CZECHOSLOVAKIA

Remember the nightmare you had during a bout of typhus?

In the nightmare, you had lost your head. (Typhus patients always make this claim.) In the nightmare, you were being tried for having betrayed science. And I condemned you to death.

In the nightmare, you also imagined that Roman Jakobson[55] had died, leaving in his place a boy at a remote railroad station. The boy knew nothing, but he was still Roman. And Jakobson's manuscripts were being burned. The boy was unable to go to Moscow and save them.

You are living in Prague, Roman Jakobson.

For two years, I have had no letters from you. And I have kept silent as though I were to blame.

Dear friend, my book *Theory of Prose*[56] has appeared. I'm sending it to you.

It is still unfinished. But that's how it was printed. You and I were like two pistons in the same cylinder. That's a fact in the life of steamships. You have been unscrewed and kept in Prague as an implement.

Dear Roman! Why work when you have no one to talk to? I

am bored to tears without you. I make the rounds of the editorial offices, I get money, I work in the movies and, in spite of everything, am on the verge of a new book.

Roman, I am studying the unfreedom of the writer. I am studying unfreedom as though it were a set of gymnastic equipment. But the streets here are full of people, so what if I do leak like a rusty pipe? The land in which I leak is my own. . . .

Roman, why don't you write me? I remember Prague. The streetlamps we put out. The bridge we couldn't afford to cross.

The Moldau—a river supposedly barred to swimmers, but full of bathing Czechs. Czech beer in litre-size steins. Kneldexi, Sonya Neiman, Pyotr Bogatyryov.[57] The bars we visited as we traversed the city. One served beer and soda, another sweet allasch.[58] I also remember sleeping on the back of a couch.

Tell me, why are we at odds? In fact, we were not.

Birds hold fast to a branch even when they sleep. People should hold fast to each other that way.

Answer me—and I'll reply with a book. How is your family life? You know, Roman, a family is like a fine, still powerful machine that the world gradually wears out. It's a shame to scrap it, but it makes no sense to start the machine up again.

Family life is impossible. It forces both husband and wife to cover their deficits every day.

A family fills every nook and cranny of the house. You have to live on the window sill, next to the little glasses of sulfuric acid.[59]

You, Roman, are real. You know Czech well and you know a lot of other languages well. You don't peddle science. You coddle it.

You know my nightmare: I am not peddling science, but dancing with it. But I don't trifle with science; I don't wear it like a necktie. And I am judging you, Roman.

When we first met on the Briks' couch, some poems by Kuzmin[60] were hanging there. You were younger than I then and I converted you to the new faith. With the inertia of your weight, you accepted it. Now you are an academician again. We are few in number. I am losing myself, as a merino loses its fleece on a thistle.

O, Roman, the pain has roused me from sleep. I have awakened.

The shadow refuses to extend me its hand.

I am flax in the field. Looking at the sky, I feel sky and pain. While you, Roman, are out on the town.

A certain little girl, two years old, used to say about all those in absentia: "He's out on the town." She had two categories: "here" and "out on the town."

"Papa is out on the town; Mama is out on the town."

During the winter, she was asked: "But where's the fly?"

It was out on the town.

But the fly was out on the window sill—stiff as a board.

We are unhappy people, Roman. We are bursting like an overstrained joint. The rivets are grinding in my heart and whitening like wrought iron as they pop out. But you are an imitator. And you a redhead! So why be an academician? They are dull, celebrating their three-hundredth anniversary.[61] They are continuous. Immortal.

The things you write now consist of data unprocessed. A lumberyard, not a building.

It is essential to seek out methods. To find a way of studying unfreedoms of a different type. And you are so useful, so intelligent—so absent; we have to make do with Vinokur,[62] celebrating his three-hundredth anniversary.

For the second time, I summon you home. I will not come after you.

ABOUT THE SECOND FACTORY

As happy-go-lucky as a man with no legs, Brik said to Eikhenbaum:

"Underneath an actor's mask is—greasepaint."

That is how Gogol's "Overcoat" was made.[63]

Apples fall to the ground in obedience to the laws of gravity—even during revolutionary holidays.

The meat was cut well—that means we sharpened the knife properly.

Don't tell us who we are. We are the stones on which the truth is sharpened.

Life goes askew if you think it exists for you.

I have a job at a film factory. Before that, I had a job at the Flax Center.

The fiber is holding as it winds into size 33. The size of my age.

I am not denying my own time. I want to understand it—how it needs me and what it means to my work.

Life.

Sometimes a scene is being shot for a movie. Everyone keeps at it relentlessly, but the pieces refuse to mesh. Nothing jells.

The long shots don't tally with the closeups. There's no movement, just dissolves.

If a bad school is good schooling, then the first factory was right.

To the second, we gave our labor and our life.

Were we sown for fiber or for seed?

THIRD FACTORY

MY NATIVE LAND

The war and revolution have already left me for other books, where there is nothing about work.

I returned from Germany with a pointer. The pointer was such a thoroughbred that she trembled constantly.

Suitcase in hand, I left behind the Berlin breakfasts in bed. A roll, butter, bad tea. . . .

Ahead lay my native land.

The border guards let me through the small republics, though they eyed my meager baggage thoughtfully. The dog trembled.

The small republics went by in a whirl. Houses covered with straw began to appear. And fields seemingly traced with a finger.

Riga is like a small fish on a big platter. Riga is too small for its harbors and warehouses.

The Latvians escorted me out of Riga. They asked me to write a sequel to Tarzan. Tarzan was to have a daughter of Latvian extraction.

In an elder forest stood a gate made of raw boards.

There hung an inscription like the one in *Pravda*:

PROLETARIANS OF ALL COUNTRIES, UNITE!

The train whistled.

My native land!

You cannot be wrong.

That is impossible. It's impossible to say: "The whole squad is out of step except for one ensign."

Moscow was a mass of signs. The people at the Vindava station were very shabby.

A mote of dust and torn paper. Such a big oasis!

And the Arabs all spoke in a familiar language.

I spent several days with my wife in Moscow—in a room vacated by the former occupants, who had left behind a pianola

45

and two squirrels.

The squirrels played together.

Some students from *Vkhutemas*[64] banged on the pianola, flashed patterns on the wall with a mirror and hoped for some sort of revelation.

It goes without saying that I should be living in Petersburg, somewhere on the other side of the Cathedral of the Transfiguration.

The grass would advance on me as it occupied the street.

I should be working on literature. Well, I do the best I can. With my own people.

I stayed in Moscow. Found a room in Pokrovsky-Streshnyov. Streetcar No. 13 goes there.

On the other side of the bridge, under the railroad, was a stone wall. The wall had three enormous cast-iron gates.

Each of the gates was bigger than those giving access to Russia.

Beyond the gates were trees, thick in the light of the streetlamp.

Beyond the pine trees was a big building, combination palace-dacha-stage set.

Surrounded by a park. The park was full of lilacs. In the spring, they were quietly broken off and taken away. Not bothered by the quiet noise, charmed by the particularly bright loveliness of the night, nightingales sang. The pond was full of slime and duckweed. The duckweed suggested cracked enamel. And the enamel was marked by the transparent swimming trails of frogs.

All this I saw in the spring, but I had arrived in the fall.

The room was full of maple leaves then. The window faced the park. All around the old furniture, covered with threadbare silk, the leaves were rustling on the floor like manuscripts.

It was beautiful. The window faced the sun. Trees.

Our room was surrounded by cold voids. A museum, black passageways, once warm, where some Circassians had lived.

The Circassians and the red stone wall and the gates were

46

supposed to save the mistress of the house from the revolution.

I got down on all fours and stuffed the cracks in the floor with rags and shredded books.

The window frosted over—no vent. The room immediately lost its beauty. We had a stove with an oven installed in the corner.

The stoveman let us down. The stove smoked.

THE TIME WENT ITS OWN WAY

I tried to detain autumn.

It was departing. It took the drapes down from the trees, threw everything on the floor, started packing.

But the birch was still green. And the willow. I refused to look at the lindens.[65] The larch was still green.

My feet rustled in the light, dry debris.

Then everything got soft and quiet. Because the ground was covered with the needles falling from the larch. The needles were followed by winter.

We dried wood on the stove. We kindled a fire in the morning and kept it going all day.

Alma the pointer got attached to us and lay all day behind the door in the darkness of the corridors.

When let in, she got warm, ate and started rapping with her hard tail. Something was boiling furiously on the stove.

I was given a big desk. I managed to scrounge a lamp.

There were a few windows in the house. There was the stone wall. Statues in their niches, snow on the bushes.

As far as electricity, telephone service and bathing facilities go, well, there was an outhouse a good two hundred yards from the house.

It was quiet.

The trees had been planted haphazardly.

47

The last owner had made the house resemble a castle by erecting a superstructure made of boards. With the moon at its back, it did look like a castle.

We had a well.

Don Quixote might well have stood guard here. It was a strange and never even remotely real life.

I am no stranger to smoke.

Quiet and fat, I ran around in a shiny black jacket. The city was far away.

The inside of the streetcar was completely covered with a shaggy steam that stuck to the walls, but I was not overcooked.

The windows were deeply incised with inscriptions.

The streetcar ran from the city, emptying as it went. It ran across bridges. It entered a wooded area.

Then the hush and the yellow streetlamp at the last station.

The kind of electricity I remembered from my childhood, when it crawled on all fours.

I'd walk toward the red wall. Stars. The gates of heavy iron. The pines in the snow and the soft, warm touch of the dog in the dark corridor.

My wife was pregnant.

That winter smelled of smoke and oranges.

A man needs very little. A room with dry walls. A stove without smoke. A window with a vent. A lamp.

In my whole life, I never learned to buy dry wood.

The stove smoked.

When we went into Moscow for a week, the room caught its breath. The smoke would disappear and the room would regain its museum appearance.

The milk would freeze in its pitcher on the stove. In the middle would be a big frozen ball, floating in thick, sweet cream.

I was writing a book about modern Russian prose.

ABOUT THE FREEDOM OF ART

Nonsense galore, as in a bathhouse.

The same sort of echo.

The walls return what I said a minute before.

Everyone talks about the freedom of art nowadays.

What art requires nowadays is material.

Art fears successors. It craves destruction. The inertia of art—that which makes it autonomous—is not needed today.

This is a black year for literature. Even the dark dreariness in a yellow bathhouse with no water or in the commissary of Herzen House[66] is better, though, than the inertia of succession.

FLAX. This is no advertisement. I'm not employed at the Flax Center these days. At the moment, I'm more interested in pitch. In tapping trees to death. That is how turpentine is obtained.

From the tree's point of view, it is ritual murder.

The same with flax.

Flax, if it had a voice, would shriek as it's being processed. It is taken by the head and jerked from the ground. By the root. It is sown thickly—oppressed, so that it will be not vigorous but puny.

Flax requires oppression. It is jerked out of the ground, spread out on the fields (in some places) or retted in pits and streams.

The streams where the flax is washed are doomed—the fish disappear. Then the flax is braked and scutched.

I want freedom.

But if I get it, I'll go look for unfreedom at the hands of a woman and a publisher.

But just as a boxer requires elbow room for his punch, so a writer requires the illusion of choice.

He regards that illusion as rather powerful material.

Lev Tolstoy wrote Leonid Andreev[67] as follows:

I think you should write, in the first place, only when the thought that you want to express is so obsessive that, until you express it as best you can, it will give you no peace. All the other incentives for writing are vainglorious and, what is worse, loathesome and venal, even though associated with the main thing—the need to express oneself; they can only interfere with sincerity and the merit of the writing. That must be strenuously avoided. Second, something which is often encountered and which, it seems to me, our current writers are especially guilty of, is the desire to be special and original, to surprise and startle the reader. That is still worse than the peripheral considerations that I mentioned earlier. That rules out simplicity, and simplicity is the essential condition of the beautiful. That which is simple and artless can be bad, but that which is obscure and artificial must be bad. Third, haste in writing. That is not only harmful but also indicative of the absence of any genuine need to express the thought in question. Because, if there is such genuine need, the writer will spare neither effort nor time to bring his thought to full definitiveness and clarity. Four, the desire to respond to the tastes and demands of the majority of the reading public at a given time. That is especially harmful and destroys at the outset the whole significance of what is being written. The significance of each verbal work lies only in the fact that it is not openly didactic, like a sermon, but that it opens to people something new and previously unknown to them, something essentially contrary to what the general public considers beyond dispute.[68]

Here the discussion seems to be about freedom.

But, in fact, what is being discussed here is not freedom, but the law of contradiction.

The Decadents contended with their material.

Tolstoy chose other material.

His whole ideology, his Tolstoyanism, his artistic structure were aimed at creating contradictions to the way the time thought.

Tolstoy no longer offends us, but for Saltykov-Shchedrin, *Anna Karenina* was a novel about the everyday activities of the urogenital organs.[69]

Without Tolstoyanism, Tolstoy could have never worked in this vein.

Tolstoy's simplicity, as is evident in "The Cossacks," is negative and indebted to art. To Circassians with daggers. To Pushkin, Lermontov, Marlinsky.[70]

I looked for freedom all around,
But the freedom promised I never found.[71]

They sing that tune in the villages. Or used to. Now they are ordered to sing about how things have fallen into place, or, at least, about how a place to put things now exists.

That is impossible for those of us in art.

That still doesn't mean that we need freedom of art. Lev Tolstoy would not have written *War and Peace* had he not been a gunner. Inside his own house, he moved in other directions, leaving the peripheral out of his books. If the line simply continues without being crossbred with the non-esthetic fact, nothing is ever created.

At the moment, there are two alternatives. To retreat, dig in, earn a living outside literature and write at home for oneself.

The other alternative is to have a go at describing life, to conscientiously seek out the new society and the correct world view.

There is no third alternative. Yet that is precisely the one that must be chosen. An artist should avoid beaten paths.

The third alternative is to work in newspapers and journals every day, to be unsparing of yourself and caring about the

51

work, to change, to crossbreed with the material, change some more, crossbreed with the material, process it some more—and then there will be literature.

In the life of Pushkin, the one clearly unnecessary thing was D'Anthes' bullet.

But terror and oppression are necessary.

A strange business. The poor flax.

You see, the artist doesn't produce an orderly arrangement of happiness. He produces a product. Here's a quotation from Tolstoy:

> Esthetic enjoyment is enjoyment of the lowest caliber—for the reason that the greatest esthetic enjoyment leaves dissatisfaction. Moreover, the greater the esthetic enjoyment, the more dissatisfaction it leaves. You keep wanting something more and more. Endlessly. Complete satisfaction is obtained only from moral goodness. That is the source of complete satisfaction. Nothing more is wanted or needed.[72]

That is Tolstoy speaking.

He, like many others, wanted a different kind of esthetic, something instructive and beneficial.

It was not to be had. But the struggle for it created works of literature.

The works that resulted, however, were completely different. Art processes the ethics and world view of a writer and liberates itself from his original intention.

Things change when they land in a book.

Take Babel,[73] for instance, who led me to the first selection from Tolstoy; Babel's all for freedom.

A very talented man, too.

I remember the late Davydov[74] in a certain comedy. He removed the top hat from his head carefully in order not to mess up his hair.

That is how Babel treats his talent. He doesn't swim around

in his book.

Change your biography. Make use of life. Break yourself over your knee.

Avoid nothing except stylistic sangfroid.

We theoreticians have to know the laws of the peripheral in art.

The peripheral is, in fact, the non-esthetic set.

It is connected with art, but the connection is not causal.

But to stay alive, art must have new raw material. Infusions of the peripheral. The destiny of the writer.

"Why did you hurt your leg?" Freud asked his son.

"Why did you have to catch syphilis, you fool?" one man asked another.

As for me, I need a destiny for the third factory.

But plot devices are lying at my door like the copper spring of a burned-up couch. Dilapidated devices, not worth fixing.

Let's take, for example, the rather widely known plot about the hero who has to overcome a series of obstacles in order to attain the room that holds his beloved.

In this, its archetypal form, we see a plot of the stepped type,[75] based on a series of impediments.

But in subsequent variants, this plot takes the following form: the hero, having attained his goal, falls asleep from exhaustion.

If the archetypal plot is represented by the schema $a^1 + a^2 + a^3$, then the subsequent variant comes out binomial, with all the obstacles represented or indicated by the letter "a" and the denouement by the letter "b." In other words, the archetypal plot is based on the inequality that distinguishes the "a" terms. In the subsequent variant, all the obstacles are perceived as a single entity and the plot inequality is derived from the unexpectedness of the denouement.

At the moment, we are experiencing an epoch in which plot form has lost its palpability. Plot form has receded from the conscious mind, just as in language, grammatical form has ceased to be palpable.

A CASE INEPTLY PLEADED BY ME

There are debts that must be paid. Unwritten, as yet, is the history of Russian literature.

But no one will publish us. They dispute our point of view. But the issue here is not us but the material and that issue is being lost in the dispute. While disputing our point of view, they appropriate our terminology. And they incorporate misconceptions into textbooks. However, we are wrong on all counts but one—we are craftsmen, we know our stuff, and when we feel like it, we will write a book ourselves.

But meanwhile, the formal method has been reduced to a set of books. One more school in the history of Russian ethnography. No, not for that did we break life over our knees. We are not spring crops, but winter crops. The first signs of green will appear any minute. Even a skimpy pasture keeps the cattle alive.

But it is essential to avoid heroism. Our botany needs no martyrs. We are not Marxists, but if that utensil should prove useful in our household, we will not eat with our hands out of spite.

This is a difficult time for art: restoration is in the air.

Writers are not streetcars on the same circuit. From Gogol to Gogol.

Edgar Allan Poe imagined the ocean of the future completely covered with cables on pontoons.[76] People dream about the future in terms of improvement, in terms of continuation. Yet the future is revolution. In the future there will be no disputes about rent.

Let them burn bookstores and ban books if they must! Anything is better than a Red Restoration. What if they don't understand art! The raw material of chocolate is far from sweet, ore makes no clang, electricity in wires gives no light.

Art in the process of change may not be palpable.

SPRING AND A BIT OF SUMMER

In the Petersburg of 1920, I was disturbed by the emptiness of the city.

A man would be urinating next to a streetlamp or in the middle of the street. Without bothering to unharness himself from the sledge he was pulling. There were no other figures in the landscape.

The streets suddenly resembled roads. The "road" that meandered haphazardly through the city was a glorified rut.

Some streets were completely choked with snow. That was a real nuisance. You wanted to pitch in and break the road yourself. In summertime, the populace was ordered to weed the streets.

I remember sailboat races on the Neva; the bridges were raised in the daytime.

It was common for the bridges to be raised in the daytime. Something or other would approach from below, give a whistle, and the bridge would be raised.

I was there once when the Nicholas Bridge was lowered informally: two or three men among those who were waiting dropped down, found the machine and started turning it by hand. Down came the bridge.

For me, a city dweller, that was very strange, like giving the heart a nudge to make it go.

Whenever a bridge was raised for several hours in the daytime, people accumulated. . . .

When the bridge came down, it was flooded with people for a second and for that second, a sector of Petersburg came alive again.

It was the same fullness seen in the sky over Sestroretsky Prospekt when spring displaces winter.

The sky fills with flocks, multitudes, specks.

As though a demonstration were being broken up or the gymnasium students were running to Kamennoostrovsky

Prospekt from Doctor Shepovalenkov's gymnasium.

Moscow gets a different sort of spring.

At the meridian of Pokrovsky-Streshnyov, spring comes like this: the snow melts. Ground appears.

Then, more often than not, snow falls again.

At Eastertime, I had hardly managed to gather some leaves of ivy when winter erupted again. We took down the enormous storm windows anyway. Our storm windows were higher than the room; they went way up into special pockets.

The trees were beaded with yellow-green buds.

In the forest, or rather under the trees, the grass was stirring last year's leaves. It was growing.

Then the bird cherry bloomed in the new cold.

What shall I say about the lilacs? They were thick. Every night the nightingales tuned up so loudly that you could have taken a bead on their voices from the other side of the mountain and picked them off with artillery.

The trees, dressed for the occasion, divided the park into sections.

People took strolls, exchanged whispers, flicked their faces with the thick lilacs. Mosquitoes.

The streetcars brought Moscow to our door.

It was sweltering hot. Lines formed on Strastnaya Square. We had ice-cream vendors. Bicycles. A restaurant. A brass band right under our window.

The public stopped under our window to read the inscription "Main Museum." The voices varied.

At the entrance gate sat a ticket taker, flicking her face with a lilac branch. Mosquitoes. Alma ran to cool off.

Toward evening, the streetlamp was lit. The foliage by the streetlamp looked very thick.

At night a car would make its way through the lanes, heading for the restaurant.

WHAT THEY ARE MAKING OUT OF ME

Things are not going well for me. I live as though sus-
pended in formaldehyde. Here in Moscow, I'm not getting any
work done. Guilty dreams disturb my sleep. I have no time to
write a book.

Sterne, whom I revived, confuses me. In the process of
turning out writers, I turned into one like him.

I have a job at the Third Factory of Goskino; my job is to
revise movies. My whole head is stuffed with bits and pieces of
movies. Like the film bin in a cutting room. A peripheral life.

Maybe "ruined" is a better word. I don't have the strength
to oppose the time and maybe opposition is unnecessary.
Maybe the time is right. It has been processing me in its own
way.

The eighteenth-century novelist Smollett describes the
following situation in his novel: the hero's friend, who is British,
is teaching his students, also British, a *new, slurred pronunciation*.[77] Apparently that unconventional articulation is the
method of pronunciation now so characteristic of modern
British English; it gradually took root in England and became
the standard—for esthetic reasons.

The rolled "r's" characteristic of modern French originated
in the province of Dauphiné and there is reason to assume that
this pronunciation too began as a fad.

Even the Polish stress (its constant location in the word)
originally began as a fad.

But where did the rolled "r" come from or, for that matter,
the slurred pronunciation? I am piling digression on digression.

The distinction between the school of *Opoyaz* and the school
of Aleksandr Veselovsky[78] lies in the fact that Veselovsky views
literary evolution as an imperceptible accumulation of slowly
changing phenomena.

If Veselovsky sees that two moments in the history of a plot
differ from one another rather sharply, he will, if unable to locate

the transitional moment, assume the existence of a missing link.

I assume that a plot develops dialectically, spurning its original form and sort of parodying itself. Veselovsky now and then comes close to the truth when he asserts that a certain artistic device might reflect an actual social custom, but such a solution to the problem strikes me as inadequate.

In brief, I see the matter in this way: change can and does take place in works of art for non-esthetic reasons—for example, when one language influences another, or when a new "social demand" appears. Thus a new form appears in a work of art imperceptibly, without registering its presence esthetically; only afterward is that new form esthetically evaluated, at which time it loses its original meaning, its pre-esthetic significance.

Simultaneously, the previously existing esthetic construction ceases to be palpable; its joints become calcified, so to speak, and fuse into a single mass.

AN EXPERIENCE THAT I HAD

I am afraid to yield to my time. Everything might turn out well and suddenly I would find myself part and parcel of the "better-with-no-legs" contingent.

I want to make of the time my destiny. I want to make contact with it through the cultivation of my craft, as when two nomadic hordes make contact. To forge a new language.

Meanwhile, youth has been quaffed. Result? A burned mouth. What do I do? I work at the factory. I read screenplays. And I ponder my destiny, 75% defined. You get used to a life with no events.

But even events deceive a man. I was just talking to a woman from the Aldan. She had gone there from Yakutsk to have a look.

Some people had been traveling from the Zeya to the Aldan on foot.[79] The Orochan guides had abandoned them. These people were starving, eating leaves and walking two kilometers a day. They decided to cast lots. There were eighty-six of them. One was to be eaten. The lot fell to a young Russian. But an old Tatar died just then from a heart attack. Overexcited by the outcome. So he was eaten.

Then they reached the Aldan. They staked out their miniscule claims. They started clearing the forest. Panning gold. The Aldan turned out to be just another job.

The Tatar was not the only one whose excitement proved premature.

Experience is instructive. And after you make love to her, the woman looks at you and says, "Thank you." Though you never said, "I love you."

A hell of a lot of dust has settled at the factory!

There are thirty-six klieg lights—we call them "Jupiters"—hanging in the studio. And four mercury stations. Films are rarely shot. There is much waiting in the corridor. Life is sparsely sown.

There is no wind pressure.[80]

A bird is carrying me. I feed it with my flesh. Out of habit. Shank, brisket, ribs. Take my heart, too, bird. And don't bother to say "Thank you."

The cutting room at the factory smells of lozenges. And you are not supposed to change the destiny of the film very much.

The smell of lozenges comes from pear oil,[81] which is used to splice the film. Female assistants do the splicing. An unhealthy line of work. The movie is wound onto rewinds; when it runs, the frames flash by like the pines on the road to the Aldan.

But I know this—my craft is wiser than I am.

LETTER TO TYNYANOV[82]

Dear Yury, I am writing you this letter not now, but last winter: these letters, then, commemorate the local winter.

I'll begin not with the business at hand, but with some information about who has gained weight and who is playing the violin.

I am the one who has gained weight. It is late at night. I have already crossed the threshold of fatigue and am in the grip of something resembling inspiration. True, etched on my brain, like the address on the yard light, are two numbers. The first, consisting of one digit, is the amount of money I need. The other, consisting of two digits, is the amount of money I owe for my apartment.

The situation is very serious. Even though we have to think on the run, we mustn't stop thinking. I like very much your study on the literary fact.[83] Your idea that literature is dynamic is well taken. The study is very important—it may be a turning point. I'm no good at paraphrasing other people's thoughts. You'll write me yourself about the implications of your study, while I write you about my skill at not making ends meet.

We contend, it seems, that a work of literature can be analyzed and evaluated without departing from the literary set. In our earlier works, we gave many examples of how something regarded as a "reflection" is actually a stylistic device. We demonstrated that a work of literature is a unified edifice. Everything in it is subjected to the organization of the material. But the concept of literature changes all the time. Literature extends its boundaries, annexing non-esthetic material. This material, and the changes which it undergoes through contact with material already esthetically processed, must be taken into account.

Literature stays alive by expanding into non-literature. But artistic form carries out its own unique rape of the Sabine women. The material ceases to recognize its former lord and master. Once processed by the law of art, it can be perceived apart from its place of origin. If that makes no sense, try this explanation. With regard to real life, art possesses several freedoms: 1) the freedom of non-recognition, 2) the freedom of choice, 3) the freedom of salvage (a fact long gone in life may be preserved in art). Art converts the particularity of things into perceptible form.

Unfortunately, the Proletarian writers are laboring under the delusion that you can put things into a film without changing their dimensions.

As for me, I've put on weight. Boris is still playing the violin. He makes a lot of mistakes. One that he and I have in common is the failure to take into account the significance of the non-esthetic set.

It is also a serious mistake to use diaries to explain the way a work of literature comes into being. There is a hidden lie here—as though a writer creates and writes all by himself and not in conjunction with his genre and all of literature, with all its conflicting tendencies. Writing a monograph on a writer is an impossible task. Moreover, diaries lead us into the psychology of the creative process and the question of the laboratory of the genius, when what we need is the thing. The relation between the thing and its creator is also nonfunctional. With regard to the writer, art has three freedoms: 1) the freedom to ignore his personality, 2) the freedom to choose from his personality, 3) the freedom to choose from any other material whatsoever. One must study not the problematical connection, but the facts. One must write not about Tolstoy, but about *War and Peace*.[84] Show Boris the letter, Yury; I've been discussing all this with him. Answer my letter, just don't lure me into the history of literature. Let's stick to art. Keeping in mind that all its magnitudes are magnitudes of a historical nature.

P.S. The intensity of private life these days would almost melt a dish of ice cream.

LETTER TO BORIS EIKHENBAUM

I'm going to write you about the *skaz*. You define *skaz* as an emphasis in the narrative on the spoken word.[85]

But even if that is true, how in the world can *skaz* be viewed outside the realm of plot? Conan Doyle's *Brigadier Gerard*[86] is built on two levels: 1) an account of some exploits, 2) a parody of those exploits, motivated by *skaz*. All the exploits prove to be a mistake. The narrator is there to supply irony. We see the same thing in Leskov's "Flea."[87] That story is bolted to the fact that the flea, once shod, stopped dancing. *Skaz* makes it possible to implement a second, ironic perception of a seemingly patriotic story. So *skaz* is (at least much of the time) a plot device and cannot be viewed outside the realm of plot. *Skaz is* also used (much of the time) to ground a system of images. *Skaz* reshapes a plot, converting the groundwork of the narrative into one aspect of the plot. *Skaz* is not the issue. Lines of demarcation are not the issue. Forget about metrics, rhyme, imagery. What matters is the process.[88] I am not being precise. But all our work has to do with the marshaling of devices, with the avoidance of categories like matter and energy, though we might concede that there is a thermal equivalent for each unit of work. Vinogradov[89] fails to understand this.

An Explanatory Note

What is this letter doing here?

In Denmark there is a city called Copenhagen. That is where Andersen[90] lived. The country is so small that passengers riding its trains probably get only half a ticket.

At that time, the streetlamps of Denmark were being converted from oil to gas.

"Get away, get away from the streetlamp, for God's sake," said Gogol in his classic tale "Nevsky Prospekt" . . . "and walk by quickly, as quickly as possible. And consider yourself lucky if it only takes a notion to spill its stinking oil on your elegant frock coat."

But, in addition to its other qualities, the streetlamp was obviously a romantic. Particularly after it was replaced by a gas light. The retired streetlamp was given a present by the stars. If you lit a wax taper in it, it turned into a magic lantern (sort of like the cinema).

But the rain gave it another present . . . "If you get fed up with everything," it said, "make a wish and you will crumble into dust."

The streetlamp fell into the hands of a night watchman—a hero of labor on pension. The streetlamp loved the night watchman and wanted to serve him as a cinema. The night watchman loved the streetlamp and sometimes fed it some oil. But why light a candle in a streetlamp?

The streetlamp made the rounds of the editorial offices. . . .

It said: "No, I am no cinema—I'm a projector." I know nothing about illuminating rooms—I'm a critic. . . .

I'm fed up with my wit. Wit is a juxtaposition of the incongruous. I am an innovator in art. . . .

With nowhere to glow. So I have lit a candle for myself here in the middle of this book.

As far as objective reality is concerned, it certainly does determine consciousness.

But in art it often runs counter to the consciousness. My brain is busy with the daily grind. The high point of the day is morning tea.

And that is too bad: some artists shed their blood and semen. Others urinate.

Net weight is all that matters to the buyer.

LETTER TO LEV YAKUBINSKY[91]

I, my friend, am not about to become a hard-and-fast Marxist and I advise you to follow my example. In literature study, the firing line is preferable to the Party line. A pun, needless to say. And what is a pun? The intersection of two semantic planes at one verbal sign. The point of the game is to create a sensation of semantic incongruity. Take the following thought. "You have nice hair," I said to a certain journalist.

"You mean hairs, not hair," he replied.

"Hairs," it so happens, is improper, referring to regions other than the head. That man was not very bright and he confused the two doublets.

A synonym seeks a destiny of its own, a meaning of its own. Compare the conversation about synonyms in Fonvizin's *Minor*. See also phrases like *"dushevnoe ne ponimaet dukhovnogo"* and Andrei Bely's assertion that the words *"miatel'"* and *"metel'"* do not have the same meaning.[92]

You linguists (Marr,[93] at any rate) talk about this; your thought could presumably be formulated as follows: a doublet leads to the creation of a new notion (the history of language bears this out, as a general rule). Respond to that. But is it true that you've studied numerals? Because the numbers "one, two, three" probably appeared later than the notion "single, double, triple." Then, too, is five the basis of the system or three? Keep in mind the system of *altyns*[94] and dozens. In the egg business, "twelve dozen" is called a "big hundred"; to seminarians (Pomyalovsky),[95] a "big heap" (of buttons) is twelve times twelve. The units of measurement used in the tanning business are the gross and multiples of forty.

A "big hundred" is the duodecimal system masked by the decimal system.

What am I driving at? I'll tell you. We need to study not protolanguage or even language in general, but language in connection with its production—above all, in those places where the phenomena in question survive. That is a rather brash statement for a non-linguist. You are studying protolanguage, but are you certain that the attitudes toward the word, the aural conditions, the substance of the laws of the word are not themselves changing? It is not just words that change: so do the attitudes toward them. I am certain, for example, that a word, in the course of its life, passes through a stage when the orientation is toward form and cases; likewise, the loss of cases was in its time a game resembling the phenomenon of humorous slang.

Lev, my friend, like you, I live on the eighth floor and members of the Komsomol come to see me gasping for breath. Our cat, while perched on the window, made the mistake of looking down and promptly plunged to the pavement from dizziness. The curve of fatigue is a good thing: at first, it diminishes work, but then right behind fatigue, and just before exhaustion, comes inspiration. I believe in your inspiration. I expect to hear from you.

ENVY BAY

It was half past eleven.

"In winter," I said to Nightingale, "the Old Believers of Lake Peipus kill their fish by rapping them on the head with a stick. They say that makes a fish open its gills; then it freezes and looks more appetizing to the customer.[96] I'm freezing, Nightingale. Do you have any idea how I will look to the customer?"

"As far as catching fish goes," I heard, "there are other ways. Read, for example, how the Papuans do it:

'Tui came out from behind the trees along the shore and watched the undulations of the fish. Suddenly the fish, probably cruelly pursued by an enemy, rushed toward the shore. With several leaps, the Papuan landed in their midst. The water there was a little above his knees and the bottom, of course, was clearly visible. Suddenly the Papuan made an energetic leap

65

and one of the fish was caught—caught by the one-foot method. First he squeezed the fish with his foot, then he puffed it out, clutched between the first and second toes of his foot. . . .'[97]

"As far as what you will look like goes, I advise you first of all to shave. One can shave very nicely with a piece of bamboo heated in a coal fire, then split. There's also another way: with a piece of glass."

But I've forgotten to tighten the coordinates of time and space in my story.

Let's begin, therefore, not with them, but with a point of departure.

In old French houses, people used to leave passageways in the walls for cats. These passageways went from room to room and from floor to floor.

In the name of a small group of people who don't know how to eat in dining rooms and, in general, don't know how to spend money on useful things and who therefore eat rolls on the street or else satisfy their hunger (if they have no family) with other people's pastry (after which they feel queasy all day long from the sour whipped cream), I turn to mankind for permission to walk along such passageways (for cats).

This story will, of course, be about something else. Let's begin with the coordinates.

It was May.

The flags on the masts of the ships at the Nicholas Bridge were flapping in the air.

In the empty streets, the wind was flapping placards the size of a city square.

The city was being cut and torn to pieces.

The placards, masts and city were beautiful.

People were shooting into the air with cheerful, urgent shots.

I was going my own separate way across Equality Bridge and thinking that it was now May 1 and the bridge was still

66

called Trinity, but it would be called Equality Bridge within only two years.

I was going to see Nightingale. Nightingale ran an antique shop and sat under a sign which said "The Cheerful Native."[98] The native was being cheerful all by himself.

He had a large room on the seventh floor.

A green cloth curtain, which a moth had devoured by the time I requested it to make myself some trousers, closed off a niche in the room—like a bay.

The large room was equipped with pictures, Ukrainian rugs, two small white elephants, and fiendishly cold weather. (The elephants were enamel. The size of a dog.)

The cold continued even in the bay behind the curtain.

It broke off only at the sofa, where, under a sealskin coat, began a warm climate.

In the corner was a fireplace, where, with the help of torn-up boxes, coffee was sometimes made by Jack—nicknamed the Witless.[99]

Witless Jack went around in ageless checked pants, which have been preserved on him even to the present day.

On that day, however, it wasn't cold; I touched up this passage with cold by mistake.

It was May.

Let's begin at the beginning.

Not with the cat, of course. It was winter.

The streets were trampled only down the middle.

A sledge was scraping along.

Jack the Witless had dragged onto Trinity Bridge a sledge with a small tile stove and seventy pounds of coal.

Jack was a talented and hard-working man, but had no particular job.

Untrustworthy and unselfish—but unselfish for lack of anything better to do.

And so only now do I reach the freezing cold which ended under the fur coat.

The owner of the space under the fur coat was Nightingale.

He was forty years old, but looked nineteen.

He had torn a knee ligament doing a native dance.

He was used to a warm climate.

He lay under the fur coat reading about travels in the Pacific Ocean and paraphrasing Jules Verne for us.

"You lie, Nightingale," I replied, catching my breath for a long digression: "there's no such thing as a warm climate! Your Papuans shave with bamboo and no soap and they freeze."

"I'll quote it to you:

'It was curious to see how the Papuan, lacking a suitable costume for the temperature, brought with him a primitive, but rather portable, stove—that is, a thick smoldering log. When he wanted to get warm, he transferred the log from one part of his body to the other and held it against his chest or put it first on one side, then on the other, or held it between his legs.' "[100]

"You call that life?"

"It's only in the mornings and in New Guinea," replied Nightingale. "But there are islands where it's always warm. These fine, useful islands, unfortunately, are sometimes destroyed by earthquakes.

"In these countries, people don't wear warm leggings or crave shoes. On one such island a missionary came and told how in his country it was so cold that water got as hard as a rock, so the missionary was put in prison for telling a lie and his story was confiscated.

"Now these islands have been ruined. Phosphate deposits were found on them and so assiduously have they been worked that the islands will probably be hauled away in toto.

"One hundred and twenty years ago, these islands were just being discovered.

"The ships had sails and men sailed them rejoicing that wind was cheap and the earth round.

"Gray rats sailed with the Europeans and also discovered

the world. . . ."

"It was intervention," I muttered under the fur coat.

Nightingale heard, but couldn't stop.

His wind was cheap to him; it blew on account of the difference between the temperature in the large room and the temperature under the fur coat. . . .

"The ships went in groups of two or three," continued Nightingale. "The men mutinied and boarded their own vessels by approaching them at night in sloops. Flocks of native dugouts came sailing toward them.

"The dugouts went with the wind; on them were the cabins of the black seafarers. The savages shot at the ship arrows sharpened on coral. The Europeans answered them with cannon fire and subjugated the islands. . . ."

I raised the fur coat a little and Nightingale stopped talking. Then I began:

"It was intervention. They sailed and they prevailed. Do you remember how the Russians discovered the Kurile Islands? They discovered the islands; on the islands were natives. The natives were seized and flogged. And then, Nightingale, out of grief they hurled themselves into the ocean and drowned. Whole tribes screamed and wept in terror."

"I'll tell you," replied Nightingale, "about an intervention that was unsuccessful."

The Russians were sailing in the Pacific Ocean. They were setting sail from Petersburg. From the Mining Academy. The water was dirty, as if house painters had been washing their brushes in it.

The ship sailed past Kronstadt, past Dago Island, mercantile Copenhagen, the windy North Sea and past England out into the ocean. And there the wind became warm and steady.

And so the ship sailed. The crew was from Novgorod.

The course was straight and the compass needle didn't change its angle with the path of the frigate. Naturally, it was a frigate with young officers, who argued in the wardroom about the revolution.

69

Not the October and not the February, but the old French one, which was then young, like the English strike.

They argued about the "social contract," about natural law and the free man.

They also talked about women.

Those conversations I'm scratching out.

Islands seemed to break off the ocean floor and bob to the surface.

The sea had already been visited and these islands were already secured on maps with meridians and parallel circles.

The ship was supposed to discover a new continent or, if worse came to worst, an island in order to name it "Count Mordvinkinland."

That was the mission of the expedition.

Mordvinkin was the new lover of the empress.

It had also been decided to discover a Tsarevich Paul Strait, an Alexander Bay and a Mount Count Potyomkin, not less than 14,000 feet high.

All this had to be discovered and annexed to the district of Kherson. On the third day's voyage from the last island marked on the map, the ship ran into seaweed. There it stood, seemingly trussed up in green snow.

Four days the sailors fretted.

On the fifth day, they got through the seaweed. On the sixth day a sailor sitting on the mast cried, "Land, ho!"

"Mordvinkin Island" had been discovered.

It was a rather large island—either that or a whole group of them.

It was essential to confirm only whether there was a Tsarevich Paul Strait.

Mount Potyomkin was already visible.

Soft. In the fog.

With a collapsed summit.

It was like the felt hat of Witless Jack.

Witless Jack, bribed by the mention of his hat, crawled out from under the fur coat and, building a fire with fragments from the neighboring two-story house (corner of Kamennoostrovsky Prospekt), made some Arabian coffee, which is unusual in that even in its country of origin it is never encountered with sugar.

We drank the coffee.

Jack returned to us and stretched out his long and checked legs next to me.

"It was extremely warm," continued Nightingale. "The cannons sprayed sunbeams and threw golden sparklers on the sails."

The black sides of the frigate boiled like pitch.

A gray cat, trying to run across the molten deck, squeaked and licked its burned paws with a dry tongue.

The white tail of the foam, held high, ran alongside the rudder of the ship.

A white belt.

White foam, scraggly as a bear, and chrysanthemums, shaggy as the sheepdog in Pokrovsky-Streshnyov, wrapped around the island.

The wreath hissed and crackled, paying no attention to the ship flying the tsar's flag.

The foam, curving, pursued the frigate.

The frigate circled the island; for a minute, a strait appeared, but the white wreath hissed and crackled.

Count Mordvinkin Island was inaccessible.

A launch, brother to the granddad of the Russian fleet, was dispatched; it joyfully broke to pieces in the breakers.

Meanwhile the islands had to be annexed.

Then two orderlies and one ensign were ordered to take an astrolabe in their teeth and swim to the island. . . .

"Sharks?" Jack inquired tersely.

"Because of the sharks, the sailors were ordered to swim from the other side of the ship," answered Nightingale.

The frigate cruised all day around the inaccessible island.

Then the light gave out.

In the sky innumerable, unfamiliar stars congregated as if

by chance.

The waves shattered into gleaming spray.

Like the tail of a comet, the water behind the rudder burned.

All in all, it wasn't bad: a tropical night had set in. . . .

"Cancer or Capricorn?" I asked.

"Capricorn and extra warm!" answered Nightingale.

"And would there be sugar?" someone wondered.

At that moment the electricity over us began to turn yellow and degenerate.

The windows emerged from the walls.

"Morning," continued Nightingale, "was beautiful."

A pleasant, gentle wind was blowing.

The sailors didn't return.

At 6:35, on the other side of the breaker, appeared some specks—more than three in number.

By 7 o'clock, the frigate was surrounded by naked savages, cheerful and stalwart.

They floated, sitting on tree stumps.

The color of their skin wasn't very dark.

And three of them were absolutely pale.

"Nails," they shouted as they floated up to the frigate, "nails!"

A ladder was lowered and the three palefaces, the ensign and the two sailors climbed on board.

They had a tired and happy appearance.

"What's ashore?" asked the captain.

"Natural man à la Rousseau," replied the ensign.

"Naked muzhiks," said the ensign.

"Captain," reported the ensign, "today there's a full moon; the tide will be especially high; there's one place where we can pull the frigate through by using the sloops as tugs."

"You can go," uttered the captain.

The ensign ran to the ship's carpenter and bought up all his nails.

Within a few hours, the frigate stood peacefully off the

luxuriant shore, separated from the ocean by the hissing fur of the surf.

Within a few more hours, the crowd of savages had climbed on board.

They were terrified by the cannons and the unfamiliar people and they were hesitant about going on deck.

The cheerful ensign wrapped a rope around himself. Holding on to the rope, the savages decided to follow him. They were laughing and terrified.

They accepted bits of cloth with delight and listened to "So Glorious Is Our Lord," which was played on the clavichord.

The captain went ashore and, in the middle of the village, read a paper about annexation.

One thing remained—to smash the idols. Unfortunately, no idols could be located.

It was very warm and fine.

The savages actually did turn out to be black muzhiks.

They broke the land into clods with the help of sharp sticks; then broke up the clods with narrow spades.

"We call this," said a sailor from Novgorod, "mattocking the field."

The village wasn't like ours but all wattled.

The huts stood on tall piles.

Across the street had been placed wattle fences about fifteen feet high.

"They're blocking the street," said the officers.

"Not at all, your highness," protested the sailor, "they did it because the wind. . . ."

"Nightingale, skip the dialogues," I advised.

The sailors wandered around the island all day.

Everything there was done without rushing, since the day was long.

It takes the Polynesians two days to cut down a tree with a stone ax tied to a handle with rawhide straps.

There are even axes made from pieces of brittle shell.

They have all the sugar you want: cane—you just chew to

your heart's content.

Like us, they have no matches. . . .

"Don't you remember, Nightingale," we protested, "that in two years we'll have NEP?"

"Ah, I did forget."

"They'll be spared an NEP. They hold their fire."

It's said that they also set fire in the forest to trees rotten at the top; the trees burn slowly; the savages light cigarettes from them and use them to tell time.

It's said that if the trees are unsuccessfully chosen and burn too quickly, then a whole tribe can die from premature old age.

For money they don't use food rations, as we do, but bundles of mats.

The sailors walked around the villages and marveled. The officers argued about Rousseau.

The savages laughed and said their new word—nails!!!

"Such funny people," said the astonished sailors, "they don't beat their women and they're nice to one another."

The savages looked and laughed. But they were barely dressed—in nothing but bracelets.

But at that time, in Moscow's public baths, the dressing rooms were joint.

"Nails!" shouted these stone-age people.

The savages' knives were made of bone and bamboo.

The sailors taught the people iron and glass. Broken bottles proved to be very useful: the savages used them to shave.

Soon the newcomers had dispersed among the houses as lodgers. Within two days they were all related to each other through the native women.

The Russian flag on the island was torn down by someone and made into a skirt.

"Captain," reported the beardless boatswain, who had never gone ashore, "our ship draws too little water, now that so many things have been stolen from it and carried away."

"Are the nails intact?" asked the captain.

"They're in my cabin."

"And why aren't you ashore?"

"I'm a skopets."[101]

"Really?"

But let's scratch out this scene.

The boatswain entered, but with a beard, and he didn't go ashore because he was true to his wife, who lived in Lodeinoe Pole.

And the sailors didn't return to the ship even though they were promised a flogging when they did.

People gathered from the neighboring villages and sat with them around the campfires breaking dry branches over their heads.

"The devil knows no shame," said the boatswain; "fornication is performed with a laugh."

I didn't scratch out the boatswain properly and he popped up again.

"I'll go look for the flag," said the captain and he left. . . .

"It's 1 A.M.," interrupted Rosa, a woman in green felt boots, who is now in Sicily. "Nearly one. Finish up."

"But you don't have a pass?"

"No."

"They didn't either."

"Those savages had no literature. However, they did have boards on which something was carved. You had to read those boards the way they write—from left to right, then from right to left. And that's all they knew about their own literature."

But the clock will now strike the denouement.

"It's best to go diagonally across the ice. Plot your course through the blizzard by the spire of the Admiralty."

"It was extremely warm on the island."

The captain was changing into a dinner jacket.

"Too late," said the entering skopets, whom I didn't scratch out properly and whom I couldn't make into a family man, "too late. The ship's sinking. They've pulled out all the nails!"[102]

Three minutes to go.

The patrols won't bother you.

Go across the ice.

There is an island (there are even several); on the islands sugar cane is eaten. It's warm there.

The language of the Polynesians, with an admixture of Russian words.

At one end of the village some French words have even been preserved.

There naked savages mattock the fields, but in the evening a military brass band plays. On the boulevard.

There are many nails to be seen and there is a bay, where drowned a certain boatswain who had no need of nails.

It's called "Envy Bay."

They practice crop rotation on the island.

On holidays, the villagers choose up sides and fight.

Let the hissing wreath of breakers lap and let nets of seaweed grow for hundreds of miles; let the storm rage and guard the island. . . .

"And Count Mordvinkin?"

"He was presented with a set of china. It's now for sale at 'The Cheerful Native.' "

Get going.

THE AIRPLANE FLEW LIKE A WOUNDED BEETLE

I haven't done any writing for a long time, because I was deafened by work. I'm definitely growing deaf in my right ear.

Thanks to the delightful work of writing screenplays, to the strain a fish undergoes in spawning on an asphalt floor.

I am not writing about the village just to fill space. The village is our destiny. It's impossible to heat one room in an unheated house. Our culture is bourgeois. It heated the room like an iron stove. The wood and iron are cooling in the deserted, darkened village. It will do no good to stuff a rug around the door.

I was given permission to proceed to the Don by airplane. The floor of an airplane is thicker than the one at home. It presses you upward. The two wings fly beside you like roofs. The clouds and the ground are unattractive. No esthetic experience prepares you for such foreshortening. The paths on the fields look like cracks. Much of the strange field below is trampled. From above, the river resembles a bold signature. Nothing is written on the fields. Whereas the signature of the Moscow River covers the whole page. Then Voronezh and a turn over the city and the bell towers that seemed swept to one side. We landed.

There stood a grimy car with palpitations of the heart. The plane was fastened to a stake.

The pilot was happy. True, he did weep in the restaurant while violins were playing. He said his wife had left him. But the next day he took a bath in the Voronezh River with pink soap and some kids enthusiastically soaped his back. A barracks stands in the center of town. It houses lotto. . . . It houses boredom. The playing lacks color and smell. It's worse than being back in gymnasium under a bench. Those who play are petty office workers and factory workers, "56 . . . 49 . . . ," the croupier intones. That night I had guilty dreams.

VORONEZH DISTRICT AND PLATONOV

All these rivers we studied in our geography book—the Voronezh, Bityug, Khoper, Tikhaya Sosna—do not exist. They are overgrown with rush. If you push the rush aside, the ground underneath is wet. Platonov[103] dredges the rivers. Comrade Platonov travels in a valiant trough that passes for an automobile.

The steppes are wide. The roads are full of gophers. They're not afraid of cars. You see wagons in the steppe; the wagons carry barrels of water.

This is not quite a desert: there are no camels here. But no water, either.

In some places, there is no water for forty kilometers in any direction. The desert crawls here via the ravines. The rivers are overgrown, growing dry. Altogether parched. Then wells are sunk in the riverbed.

The villages crawl toward the water and sprawl at the water's edge. Big, dull villages with as many as 15,000 inhabitants. They're called Big Stump, Dog's Wallow and other not very cheerful names.

There are villages where people stand at the well all night long with their buckets. A man and his horse must be watered there.

If you build dams across the ravines, you can keep water in them. The amount of dirt exhumed here in the last two years would rival Mount Ararat. Platonov is a specialist in land reclamation. A worker, about twenty-six years old. Blond.

The huts are made of stone, with wooden chimneys and straw roofs. The whole thing is plaited together like a bale of hay to keep it from flying asunder. The steppe is dotted with ponds. Damn fine ones you are, too! Some of the ponds extend for several kilometers. Willows are planted on their banks. Then huts are built around them. People manage.

It is cold and dark here without ponds—something like the museum building in Pokrovsky-Streshnyov.

The Don is turbid. The ravines run into it like white lizards.

The rivers here are still being dredged and straightened; the swamps are being drained and lime is spread on the land to counteract the acidity of the fields.

The Tikhaya Sosna has now been dredged.

Comrade Platonov is very busy. The desert is advancing. Water goes underground and flows there in big underground rivers.

The dams are constructed during the winters. Since the ground is frozen, fires are built on the dams at night.

78

The district is infiltrated with syphilis. The craving for it is more serious.

CHEAP MOTORS

There was an orchard and the orchard was watered. The water came from a deep well. It was channeled into wooden chutes. The chutes stood on stilts. The water ran through the chutes into big tubs. . . .

The orchard was watered, so the fruit, instead of falling, ripened. . . . The whole orchard was safe and sound. Around it grew tall stalks of oats.

Normally, there is only one way to protect an orchard in the steppe: a square of non-fruit trees. The rabbits leave them alone. This way the rabbits got the oat crop.

There should have been a motor to pump the water.

Instead it was brought from another well by a coil pump.[104] The coil ran into the water and out again, the water clinging to it.

The wheel of the spring was turned by two girls. "Given the agrarian overpopulation of the village and the famine in Voronezh," Platonov told me, "there's no motor cheaper than the village girl. She requires no amortization."

The orchard stood there, ripening. When evening came, the sun set and it got dark.

We sat on the terrace and ate an abominable dinner with the specialists in land reclamation.

Platonov talked about literature, about Rozanov;[105] he also objected to describing sunsets and writing short stories.

In the darkness, gray-legged horses neighed. Some members of the co-op were spending the night with them. They were urging the horses to breed. The gray-legged horses neighed.

The darkness was broken by the sound of the cheap motors

singing.

We went on our way.

A lad was pounding on an iron tambourine and pawing the ground with his bare feet. The girls were singing in high, pure voices. The district is infiltrated with syphilis.

One couple was dancing: the guy with the tambourine and a woman wearing a striped, calico dress.

The guy was singing *chastushki* with unbelievable words. As Platonov explained, a single being was once split into a man and a woman. Each half was supplied with distinctive features. The song dwelled on those features. They kept joining together in bizarre combinations.

The woman responded in her song. Far too primly and as though she didn't hear the tambourine.

SUBSEQUENTLY

The dams are made of dirt. The keystone of the dam, its lowest portion, is made of compressed clay. A man and his horse must be watered and the enormous villages dying of boredom and unable to work must be resettled.

Lev Nikolaevich Tolstoy said that if you look at things with an eye to describing them, you will not see them.

Platonov understood the village. I flew over it in an airplane. We didn't really hit it off. In the cockpit the pilot and I sang "Little Bricks." The airplane flew like a wounded beetle. A slanting rain went past the window.

We spent the night on the riverbank, sleeping in the plane, which we covered with a tarpaulin. We saw an orphanage. Four hundred foundlings. Three to a bed. They were suffering from malaria and bed sores. Not to mention the absence of their own destiny. Every child needs one.

These children had new names: Turgenev, Dostoevsky. . . .

80

Their diapers were marked with crosses. To keep them from being stolen. The villages are enormous—impossible to heat. There are people in them who saw the revolution. They are bored and yearn for the city. The village wants to be a city.

A crowd stood around the airplane all night long and policemen stood guard. The old people asked us, "What is on the other side of them clouds?" Them rather than those.

"Not god," replied the pilot. He argued about god and exposed the icons as fake by pointing out that the Prophet Elijah was riding in a chariot with beveled spokes. In those days, there were no lathes. The village didn't argue. It was bored and we had arrived by airplane. The village asked how much a ride would cost. And it would have collected the money for a ride from those huts with no window panes. . . .

The village is suffering from bed sores. These people are fresh from the revolution and they want a destiny of their own.

THE FIELDS OF OTHER DISTRICTS

A peaceful life. The peasant in Voronezh District quietly plows his field. With four cows. The local cattle can take it. Kalmyk cattle. Horses were lost in greater numbers during the civil war than cows.

The cows are needed for plowing. They do, however, have an aversion to heat.

But then the fields do not need my irony.

I do need the fields, though; I need real things. If I don't find some way of seeing them, I will die.

The fields in the district of Tversk are different. Enclosed. Some villages even have the twelve-field system of crop rotation. One such village has a house bearing the inscription: "Permanent U.S.S.R. Museum of the Village of Kutuzovo."

Kutuzovo found its place in the U.S.S.R. immediately and

81

thereby in the world. Electricity has been installed. The wallpaper in the huts is not darkened by smoke.

"This potato field is already a town," I was told in Likhoslavl.

The town had existed for two weeks. But socks are knitted there. Machines and money are plentiful. Also respect for the women who knit the socks.

And the singing is different.

But I was also in the vicinity of Krasny Kholm in connection with the Flax Center. Snow was falling and melting. The horse, lacking shoes, was ticklish and refused to walk on the road. . . . We traveled alongside the road. The ride was so rough that we travelled three kilometers before noticing that we had lost our right wheel. The snow on the fields looked like torn rabbit pelts.

And in those fields, where one flat rectangle succeeded another flat rectangle, lay flax. The corners of the rectangles were rounded. Snow lay on the flax.

We are flax in the field. You know that.

My own destiny has found no place in this book. My destiny ended in childhood. Life escaped through the cracks. The other rooms were not heated.

Love concealed and silenced proved unsuccessful. As things have worked out, it seems that I do have the right to cultivate my own garden. I wish to lie in the field.

A SECOND CHILDHOOD

He is now eighteen months old. Pink, round and warm. His eyes are set wide apart and oval in form. Dark eyes. He doesn't walk yet, just runs. His life is still continuous. Not made up of drops. All of it is palpable. When he runs, his little legs churn.

When we took him to the country for the summer, he liked to be held by his heels. To look at the grass.

He looked at walls; the sky he ignored. He grew. There was oakum in the walls. In town, he looked at a doll and saw its debt to man. He squeezed into a basket upside down and carried it around the room.

He tried to climb on the table. A table higher than he was.

The boy dragged the basket over to the table and climbed in, but he was no taller. The basket was right side up.

Then he turned the basket over, backed up to it on all fours and put his feet on it. Nothing worked: he couldn't get up no matter what. Within a few days, though, he had learned to climb up and reach the tabletop.

During the interim, he knocked everything off the table with a stick. Now he climbs wherever he wants by dragging a suitcase around.

He plays with the window, the stovepipe and me. He visits me every morning to check out the room and tear up a few books. He keeps growing—faster than grass in the spring.

I have no idea how he registers all the events in his life. He seems remarkable to me.

What he likes about me is my shiny skull. The time will come. . . .

When he grows up, he will, of course, not be a writer. But he will probably remember his father. His father's extravagant taste.

The way toys smelled. The way his doll Mumka was soft and compact.

But I now have a different memory of my father.

I remember: a big, bald, handsome head. Gentle eyes. A fierce voice. Strong hands with thick palms—the same hands my son has.

And the dependable heat of his forehead.

As for your father's house. As for my house, Kitik, I can tell you myself.

It is not without its ridiculous aspects. Three wicker chairs in the style of the fourteenth Ludwig. A table with eight legs. A shelf of books as rumpled as people spending the night in a railroad station.

No candelabra whatsoever. A floor that gives when you step on it. A lightbulb hastily hung from the ceiling. Enough money for one day.

THE THIRD FACTORY

Near the Bryansk Station. Bryansk Lane, No. 3. Gray gateway, red wall.

On the third floor is a commissary. Tea is drunk there. The tea sublimates time.

In micro-scenes, where time must be divided into thousandths, the shooting is sometimes done by the light of a flare. The rest of the time is filled with darkness and tea—abominable tea. It takes very little time to shoot a movie. If there were no retakes, if there were no sets to put up, a movie could be shot in a matter of hours.

But life is slow. The actors sit around in the corridor. Grow beards for their parts. Drink tea.

The dozens of lights hanging in the studio resemble gleaming bats.

The sets are made of logs. Durability counts when you run through a screenplay for the thousandth time.

The sets are in pieces. Everything the camera will see is of heavy construction. Surrounded by holes. "Lights, camera, action," shouts the director. Two minutes of shooting. The cameramen are sunburned from the light of the "Jupiters." The cameramen do their cranking from a crouching position. Both camera and cameraman give the impression of being about to pounce on the actor.

IF the chorus of lights does not produce quivering shadows.

IF the actors do all right.

Then you get not only a film but numerous cuttings, which

84

are kept in the canvas-covered bins of the cutting room.

Who will edit? Eddie Shub,[106] of course. Even if the film is a bust, she will do her job.

Americans follow the same procedure. They have more celluloid, and even Mary Pickford lies in the film bin when the celluloid is cleaned. She too drinks tea in a commissary. As a factory—the factory is right. As life—the factory is a flop.

The studio occupies three stories.

The producer's office is on the second floor.

In the corner stand two cheval glasses in gold—from the prop room. Baroque. A sinuous writing desk—*style moderne*. A chandelier—Renaissance. On the floor, an imitation Persian rug. On the walls, portraits of the most eloquent directors.

This is where I spawn.

I would like to film life in a different way—to achieve a different rhythm. I love long strips of life. Give the actors a chance to show their stuff.

Less tea, less cutting. All we can do is try.

The producer, as pink as I, listens to me and simultaneously talks on the telephone.

Sometimes a movie is faulty. Improperly shot. Nothing jells. The movements don't tally. The director has staged it badly. Then they say: "This picture goes on the shelf."

The shelf is a sort of cemetery.

During the days of film famine, the dead buried in that cemetery will be resurrected.

But never will the dead buried in our cemeteries be resurrected.

All of us are merchandise laid out in neat rows for the inspection of our time. . . . We must not die: kindred spirits will be found.

The producer rocks ever so lightly in his swivel chair. The chair creaks.

And I remember the gymnasium—some lines translated from Virgil:

> And the southern wind,
> With a quiet creaking of the masts,
> Calls us to the open sea.[107]

AFTERWORD

Take me, third factory of life!
But don't put me in the wrong guild.

Whatever happens, though, I have some insurance: good health. So far, my heart has borne even the things I haven't described.

It has not broken: it has not enlarged.

NOTES

1. In his book *Theory of Prose*, Shklovsky describes "stringing" *(nanizyvanie)* as that compositional device in which the episodes of the plot are tied together by the presence of a central character.

2. Shklovsky's only son, Nikita, born in 1924, was killed on February 8, 1945, during the last days of the war. Some poignant glimpses of him as a young man may be found in Nadezhda Mandelstam's memoirs *Hope against Hope* (New York, 1970). Shklovsky's daughter, Varvara, was born in 1926.

3. Brehm, Alfred Edmund (1829-1884), German naturalist and author of a famous multi-volume work on animal behavior. In his work, elephants are, of course, described as trumpeting.

4. A colorful, ancient street running west of the Kremlin.

5. These are lines from a poem called "Lyrical Digression" *("Liricheskoe otstuplenie")*, published by Nikolai Aseev in 1924.

6. Formerly, the Ermolev Film Studio. The second factory of Goskino was formerly the Skobelev Foundation's documentary film studio. The first factory was formerly the "Khanshonkov & Co." film studio.

7. A play by Denis Ivanovich Fonvizin, first performed in 1782.

8. Smirdin, Aleksandr Filippovich (1795-1857), Russian book dealer and publisher. He was one of the first publishers to pay royalties, which allowed writers a certain independence from the court. One way in which the Formalists attempted to compromise with the demands of the Marxists was to study the milieu of the writer and the ways in which, for example, the payment of royalties affected the development of literature. Eikhenbaum and Shklovsky later edited a major study of Smirdin's activities and influence. See *Slovesnost' i kommertsiia; knizhnaia lavka A. F. Smirdina*, by T. Grits, M. Nilitin, V. Trenin (Moscow, 1929).

9. Efros, Abram Mikhailovich (1888-1954), noted art historian and translator. The Russian adjective *zolotoobrezanyi* is a neologism that suggests *zolotoobreznyi* and refers to a luxuriously designed book of Pushkin's drawings that Efros had edited and published in the early twenties; *obrezannyi* means "circumcised" and was, according to Shklovsky, a dig at the "hygienic" quality of Efros's work.

10. Shklovsky is probably referring to the occasions when the French fleet put into St. Petersburg at the turn of the century.

11. Shklovsky later discovered that his grandfather was Latvian.

12. *Niva (Corn Field)* was a popular illustrated weekly published from 1870 to 1918.

13. The modern school *(real'noe uchilishche)* emphasized science and mathematics rather than the humanities.

14. The overcoat in Gogol's famous short story was made with a catfur collar. Shklovsky is also alluding playfully to Boris Eikhenbaum's article "How 'The Overcoat' Is Made," which analyzes the verbal material of "the overcoat." See note 63.

15. Reisner, Larisa Mikhailovna (1885-1926), beautiful Bolshevik commissar who was active in literary affairs and who fought at the front during the civil war.

16. Pavlov, Ivan Petrovich (1849-1936), famous Russian physiologist who formulated the theory of conditioned reflexes.

17. Potebnya, Aleksandr Afanasevich (1835-1891), a philologist whose studies of poetry and prose provided a point of departure for the Formalists. He viewed poetry and prose primarily as linguistic phenomena and insisted on the distinction between everyday language and literary language. His idea that words lose their freshness with the passage of time and need to be revived by the poet contributed to Shklovsky's formulation of the concept of enstrangement, though Shklovsky specifically refuted Potebnya's insistence on the accessible image as the hallmark of poetry.

18. In August, 1918, the Council of People's Commissars issued a decree that opened the universities to all applicants. Workers' Schools *(Rabfak)* were opened in early 1919 for the purpose of preparing workers to meet university standards.

19. Nyslott is now called Savonlinna; Olaf's Castle is the famous medieval fortress known as Olavinlinna.

20. Shklovsky spent a few weeks in Finland during the spring of 1922, in transit to Berlin after escaping from Russia to avoid arrest for anti-Bolshevik activities.

21. After the Bolshevik revolution, Russia acceded to Finland's demand for complete independence. But forty thousand Russian troops remained in Finland, supporting the extreme left-wing forces in that country. The so-called activists organized a Civil Guard under General Gustav Mannerheim to expel the Russian troops. Meanwhile, the Social Democrat Party, supported by the Russian troops, seized Finland. A bloody civil war ensued. With the aid of German troops, the Whites succeeded in conquering the Reds, and the war ended in May 1918.

22. This anecdote is from Tolstoy's work "What's To Be Done?" *("Chto zhe nam delat'?").*

23. For Baudouin de Courtenay, see note 37.

Meillet, Antoine (1866-1936), was a French philologist and linguist—author of numerous tracts on Indo-European and general linguistics, as well as historical grammars of Common Slavic, Old Persian, Classical Armenian, Greek, and Latin.

24. *Vesy* and *Apollon* were journals closely associated with the Symbolist movement. *Vesy* was published in Moscow between 1904 and 1909, *Apollon* in Petersburg between 1909 and 1917. *Let Us Be Like the Sun (Budem kak solntse)* was a famous collection of poetry published in 1902 by the Symbolist poet Konstantin Dmitrievich Balmont (1867-1942).

25. Ginzburg, Ilya Yakovlevich (1859-1939), sculptor noted for his realistic busts of famous Russian artists and scientists. After the revolution he produced a series of works commemorating important moments of the epoch. The last years of his life were devoted to essays and memoirs.

26. Sherwood, Leonid Vladimirovich (1871-1954). Sherwood received his training at the Moscow School of Painting, and at the Petersburg Academy of Arts, after which he studied for a year in Paris with Rodin. His pre-revolutionary work was basically realistic, with elements of impressionism. After some difficulties during the twenties, he redeemed himself with his monument to the Red Army *(The Sentry)* in 1933.

27. David Davidovich Burlyuk (1882-1967), Aleksei Eliseevich Kruchyonykh (1886-1968) and Nikolai Davidovich Burlyuk (1890-1920) were all prominent Futurists. Kornei Ivanovich Chukovsky (1882-1969) was a prominent literary critic, translator and writer of children's books. Chukovsky was one of the first critics to write about the Futurists, but his attitude, compounded of condescension and a desire to capitalize on their notoriety, offended Shklovsky.

28. In other words, the stairway is an illusion and, like the stairways in fairy tales, dissolves behind the person as he ascends.

29. Korolenko, Vladimir Galationovich (1853-1921), a popular and rather sentimental short-story writer who fought actively for reforms during the reign of Nicholas II.

30. Kulbin, Nikolai Ivanovich (1868-1917), an eccentric doctor who actively promoted the new trends in Russian art among the inhabitants of Petersburg. He wrote articles and sponsored exhibitions and lectures.

31. Evreinov, Nikolai Nikolaevich (1879-1953), noted playwright, as well as theoretician and historian of the drama.

32. This seemingly innocent set of names provides an illustration

of Shklovsky's law of contradiction—the technique whereby a writer creates parallels in order to highlight the disparities that exist in the presence of similarity. Gorodetsky, Sergei Mitrofanovich (b. 1884) was a poet closely associated with the Acmeists and their leader, Nikolai Gumilev. After Gumilev was executed in 1921, Gorodetsky published a condemnation of his former friend and disassociated himself from the Acmeist movement. Ironically, he now inhabits a building where famous victims of government repression like Gumilev have lived. Ksenya Godunov, the daughter of Boris, was strangled at the behest of Dimitri the Pretender, who succeeded Boris to the throne in 1605. Pugachyov led an insurrection against Catherine the Great, who had him executed in 1775. Novikov, Nikolai Ivanovich (1744-1818) expressed criticism of serfdom, thereby antagonizing Catherine, who retaliated by shutting down his journals periodically. She eventually had him imprisoned in 1792.

33. Gnedov, Vasily Ivanovich (b. 1890), an experimental poet nominally belonging to the Ego-Futurists, but actually closer to the Cubo-Futurists in his extreme verbal experiments.

34. Pronin, Boris, founder of the famous literary cabaret called the Stray Dog, which was frequented by the avant-garde circles of Petersburg.

35. Belenson, Aleksandr Emmanuilovich, a mediocre poet tenuously attached to the Futurist movement. He published the three miscellanies called *The Archer (Strelets)* in 1915, 1916, and 1923.

36. *Voskreshenie slova* (Petersburg, 1914). This brochure contains the contents of a speech that Shklovsky delivered at the Stray Dog cabaret in December 1913. It was an attempt to provide a theoretical explanation of Futurist poetry, which he praised for its ability to strip words and objects of their encrusted meanings and give them a new vitality. *Resurrection of the Word (Voskreshenie slova)* is usually regarded as the cornerstone of Russian Formalism.

37. Baudouin de Courtenay, Jan (1845-1925), a leading Slavic philologist and professor at the University of Petersburg; one of the originators of modern phonology.

38. See note 91.

39. Baudouin was, on the whole, disdainful of the Futurists' insistence on the primacy of sound in poetry, but he did agree to chaperone two programs which the Futurists planned in February 1914 as a rebuttal to the lecture of F. Marinetti, the Italian Futurist then visiting Petersburg. When he joined Shklovsky and Vladimir Pyast on stage for the first program, he was dismayed to see that one of them

was wearing a brocade vest made of priestly vestments, the other a necktie in a rather unusual place. Indignant, he walked out and refused to chaperone the second program. See Benedikt Livshits, *Polutoraglizyi strelets* (Leningrad, 1933), pp. 246-251.

40. Shklovsky had close ties with the right-wing SR's and served as a commissar in the Provisional Government after the February revolution.

41. The Russian army occupied Galicia briefly during September of 1914. At that time, policemen were mobilized and sent to the front. Subsequently, as dissatisfaction with the regime's conduct of the war produced a growing number of strikes and other disturbances in Petrograd, policemen were needed to keep order in the capital and were therefore exempted from duty at the front—a fact that created great resentment among the enlisted men.

42. This is "Mademoiselle Fifi," a story about a group of Prussian officers in occupied Normandy during the Franco-Prussian War. The men call their commander Fifi because of his affectations. Bored, they invite a group of prostitutes to their chateau for dinner. The occasion is rapidly becoming an orgy when one of the men proposes a toast to their victories over France. One of the women, incensed, defends French honor. The discussion grows more heated until she stabs Fifi fatally and flees. Though the Prussians hunt her far and wide, she is never caught and, after the withdrawal of the Prussian troops, eventually marries a Frenchman who admired her exploit.

43. Brik, Osip Maksimovich (1888-1945), a leading exponent of Futurism, Formalism, and LEF. Brik, Lilya Yurievna (b. 1892), sister of Elsa Triolet and mistress of Vladimir Mayakovsky.

44. Verkhovsky, Aleksandr Ivanovich (1886-1938), Minister of War during the last few months of the Provisional Government. In 1918, Verkhovsky was arrested for anti-Bolshevik activity. He was released in 1919, after seeing the error of his ways, and thereafter taught at the Frunze Military Academy.

45. This is *"Zvukovye portory,"* first published in *Sborniki po teorii poeticheskogo iazyka* (Vol. II; Petrograd, 1917) and reprinted in Volume III (Petrograd, 1919). This essay was later reprinted in *Two Essays on Poetic Language,* ed. L. Matejka (Vol. V of *Michigan Slavic Materials;* Ann Arbor, 1964).

46. The reproaches directed by Shklovsky at Brik must have had an effect. Substantial portions of this work appeared in 1927. It is called *"Ritm i sintaksis (Materialy k izucheniyu stikhotovornoi rechi)" Novyi Lef,* 3 (March 1927); 4 (April, 1927); 5 (May 1927); 6 (June 1927). It was

reprinted in *Two Essays on Poetic Language,* ed. L. Matejka (Vol. V of *Michigan Slavic Materials;* Ann Arbor, 1964). Part of the essay was translated into English in *Readings in Russian Poetics: Formalist and Structuralist Views,* ed. L. Matejka and K. Pomorska (Cambridge and London, 1971; reprinted by Dalkey Archive Press, 2002).

47. For Jakobson, see note 55; for Tynyanov, see note 82.

48. Tomashevsky, Boris Viktorovich (1890-1957), a prominent member of *Opoyaz,* known especially for his work on Pushkin. Shklovsky was scornful of Tomashevsky's book *Teoriia literatury,* which appeared in 1925, because it was merely a codification of the Formalists' view of literature and because it included basic ideas of the Formalists, such as Shklovsky's "enstrangement" *(ostranenie),* without giving credit to those who originated these ideas.

49. This is evidently Passover.

50. The word "doldrums" *(vremia glukhoe)* echoes significantly the famous 1914 poem by Blok, in which he describes the pre-war years as "doldrums" *(goda glukhie)*—a phrase that Mandelstam repeated in the first line of his novella "The Noise of Time" *(Shum vremeni'),* 1925. By applying that phrase to the mid-twenties, Shklovsky is suggesting, as elsewhere in this book, that the beneficial effects of the revolution were only temporary and that its promise has not been realized.

51. *Vzyal* appeared in December 1915. No other issues were published.

52. Shklovsky is referring to the first collection, which appeared in 1916. Two other collections followed: in 1917 and 1919.

53. Bely, Andrei (pen name of Boris Nikolaevich Bugaev) (1880-1934), famous Symbolist poet and pioneer of modernist prose. In his book *Simvolizm* (Moscow, 1910), he dealt extensively with onomatopoeia.

54. Grammont, Maurice (1866-1946), a French linguist and literary scholar; his article was called *"Zvuk, kak sredstvo vyrazitel'nosti rechi"* ("The Sound as an Expressive Vehicle of Speech"). Nyrop, Kristoffer (1858-1931), a Danish linguist and professor at the University of Copenhagen. His article was called *"Zvuk i ego znachenie"* ("The Sound and Its meaning"). Both articles were translated into Russian by Shklovsky's brother Vladimir.

55. Jakobson, Roman Osipovich (1896-1982), a leading member of the Moscow Linguistic Circle, an offshoot of *Opoyaz.* Jakobson emigrated to Prague in 1920, an act which Shklovsky strongly criticized in an open letter published in *Knizhnyi ugol,* VIII (1922), where he accused Jakobson of having abandoned his work on poetics and urged him to

return to Russia. Jakobson responded in his book *O Cheshskom stikhe, preimushchestvenno v sopostavlenii s russkim (On Czech Verse, as Compared Primarily to Its Russian Counterpart)* (Berlin, 1923), which has the terse dedication: "To Viktor Shklovsky, in lieu of an answer to his letter in *Knizhnyi ugol.*" A few weeks after attacking Jakobson's decision to emigrate, Shklovsky himself emigrated to Berlin to escape prosecution for his anti-Bolshevik activities during the Civil War. In the Fall of 1923, he was granted an amnesty and returned to the Soviet Union, stopping en route to visit Jakobson in Prague—the visit described in this letter.

56. *O teorii prozy; Theory of Prose* (Moscow, 1925; Elmwood Park, 1990). An expanded edition appeared in 1929.

57. Bogatyryov, Pyotr Grigorevich (1893-1969) lived in Berlin for a while after the revolution, then moved to Prague—apparently on a mission for the Soviet government. He lived in Prague until 1940, at which time he returned to the Soviet Union and eventually became a well-known specialist in Slavic folklore.

58. A sweet kümmel prepared with flavoring agents such as bitter almonds, angelica root, anise or orange peel.

59. When storm windows were put on, it was customary to spread cotton on the sill between the windows and to set two small glasses of sulfuric acid there to absorb moisture and keep the panes from fogging over.

60. Kuzmin, Mikhail Alekseevich (1875-1936), a Symbolist poet lacking the metaphysical dimension usually found in the Symbolists and known for the high level of his craftsmanship.

61. *Ryzhii* (translated as "redhead") also means "clown." And the figure "three-hundredth" seems not to be a random choice. In 1913, the Romanov dynasty celebrated its three-hundredth anniversary. Four years later, it was overthrown. Shklovsky is suggesting—a vain hope— that the rule of epigones may not be permanent.

62. Vinokur, Grigory Osipovich (1896-1947), linguist and literary critic, professor at Moscow University from 1942 to 1947. Vinokur had repeatedly criticized Shklovsky for abstracting literature from its historical context. See G. Vinokur, *"Novaia literatura po poetike," LEF,* 1 (March, 1923), p. 242. See also his article in *Russkii sovremennik,* 3 (1924), p. 264.

63. Eikhenbaum, Boris Mikhailovich (1886-1959), a prominent Russian Formalist who made major contributions in the areas of *skaz,* verse theory and literary history. Shklovsky is referring to Eikhenbaum's famous article "How 'The Overcoat' Is Made," which was apparently inspired by a chance remark of Brik's. Eikhenbaum's article

appeared in Volume III of *Studies of the Theory of Poetic Language* (Petrograd, 1919). An English translation appeared in *The Russian Review* (October, 1963) and in Robert A. Maguire's book *Gogol from the Twentieth Century* (Princeton, 1974). See also Note 85.

64. *Vysshie xudozhestvennye tekhnicheskie masterskie* (Higher Artistic and Technical Studios). A free-wheeling public institution founded in Moscow in 1918 for the study of painting, sculpture, architecture, ceramics, metalwork, textiles and typography.

65. They evoked painful memories of Berlin, where Shklovsky spent a miserable year in exile—experiences that he described in his epistolary novel *Zoo, or Letters Not about Love* (Berlin, 1923). An English translation of this novel appeared in 1971 (reprinted by Dalkey Archive Press, 2001).

66. A center for writers and journalists founded in 1920.

67. Andreev, Leonid Nikolaevich (1871-1919), a popular writer who depended excessively on sensational effects derived from the themes of sex and death.

68. Tolstoy wrote this letter to Andreev on September 2, 1908. See L. N. Tolstoy, *Polnoe sobranie sochinenii* (90 volumes; Moscow, 1935-58), LXXVII, 218-220.

69. Saltykov-Shchedrin, Mikhail Evgrafovich (1826-1889), a well-known satirist and leader of the radical intelligentsia. When the first sections of *Anna Karenina* began to appear in 1875, he wrote P. V. Annenkov a letter in which he referred to "Tolstoy's novel about the conditions most conducive to the everyday activities of the genitals. That upsets me terribly. It's terrible to think that it is still possible to build a novel on nothing but sexual motives. That strikes me as base and immoral." See M. E. Saltykov-Shchedrin, *Sobranie sochinenii* (12 volumes; Moscow, 1965-1971), XI, 633.

70. Pushkin, Aleksandr Sergeevich (1799-1837). Lermontov, Mikhail Yurievich (1814-1841). Marlinsky, pen name of Bestuzhev, Aleksandr Aleksandrovich (1797-1837). Shklovsky has in mind Pushkin's *The Captive of the Caucasus* (1822), Lermontov's *A Hero of Our Time* (1840), and Marlinsky's *Ammalat Bek* (1832).

71. Lines from a *chastushka:*   *Plo slobode ia poshel,*
                                     Tam svobody ne nashel.

72. This passage comes from Tolstoy's *Diaries* for 1896. See Tolstoy, *PSS*, LIII, 104.

73. Babel, Isaak Emmanuilovich (1894-1941), master of the short story, known especially for his Red Cavalry cycle.

74. Davydov, Vladimir Nikolaevich (pseudonym of Ivan

Nikolaevich Gorelov) (1849-1925), a famous actor known especially for his work in Chekhov's plays.

75. Stepped form, a term coined by Shklovsky in his work on literary theory, refers basically to the system of parallels and conceptually related episodes by which a narrative moves forward.

76. This is a reference to one of Poe's experiments in science fiction, "Mellona Tauta," whose hero describes crossing the ocean by balloon in the year 2848 (April 1).

77. This is a reference to Smollett's novel *The Adventures of Roderick Random*, 1748. The teacher in question proves to be a Scottish gentleman who claims to be teaching English pronunciation by a radical new method. The dialect is mostly unintelligible to the hero and seems, in fact, to have little connection with modern British pronunciation.

78. Veselovsky, Aleksandr Nikolaevich (1838-1906), an outstanding scholar in the field of comparative literature. His studies, with their emphasis on the development of archetypal devices and plots, profoundly influenced Shklovsky and provided a groundwork for the work of the Russian Formalists. Shklovsky, while admiring his work, objected to his insistence on the origin of forms in social customs and to his view of literary development as a process of gradual evolution.

79. These are rivers in Eastern Siberia, the distance between them being about 200 miles. Gold was discovered on the Aldan in 1923, which is probably when the events described took place.

80. This is a reference to a story about the peasant who complained to an old man that St. Nicholas had ruined his crops by providing the wrong kind of weather. The old man, who proved to be St. Nicholas, took offense and told the peasant to make his own weather. Another crop failure, even worse, resulted. When St. Nicholas returned, he asked the peasant about his procedures: had he included wind, for instance? The peasant had omitted wind for fear that it would beat down the grain. St. Nicholas then informed the peasant that neither rye nor wheat goes to seed without wind. Shklovsky tells this story in *Khod konia (Knight's Move)* (Berlin, 1923), pp. 12-14. It is apparently his own variation on the Russian folk tale called "Elijah the Prophet and St. Nick."

81. Amyl acetate.

82. Tynyanov, Yury Nikolaevich (1894-1943), a prominent Russian Formalist, known especially for his brilliant comparative study "Gogol and Dostoevsky," 1921, and for his remarkable book on verse theory, *The Problem of Verse Language*, 1924.

83. This is Tynyanov's landmark article *"O literaturnom fakte"*

("Concerning Literary Fact"), published in *LEF*, 2 (1924), pp. 100-116, and reprinted in Tynyanov's collection *Arkhaisty i novatory (Epigones and Innovators)* (Leningrad, 1929), pp. 5-29. In this article, Tynyanov suggested that a critic was obligated to do more than merely catalogue the devices in a work of literature, as Shklovsky had come perilously close to suggesting, but that it was also important to examine the function of each device. The functions of devices change. Then, applying Shklovsky's conception of literary change, he said that literary genres once peripheral, such as memoirs and diaries, were now moving into the ascendant position. The public was demanding literature with less artifice. This article was dedicated to Shklovsky, who clearly endorses this more sophisticated approach.

84. In this paragraph, Shklovsky is referring to Eikhenbaum's book *The Young Tolstoi (Molodoi Tolstoi)*, 1922, of which Gary Kern published an English translation in 1972. In that book, Eikhenbaum relied heavily on Tolstoy's diaries, which Shklovsky considers a violation of the principles of the formal method. Eikhenbaum continued working on Tolstoy the rest of his life—work that resulted in a long unfinished monograph, *Lev Tolstoy* (2 vols.; Leningrad, 1928-31), republished by the Wilhelm Fink Verlag in 1968. After the appearance of Shklovsky's book on Tolstoy in 1928, Shklovsky and Eikhenbaum continued their debate in a series of interesting letters published in Shklovsky's book *Podenshchina* (Leningrad, 1930), pp. 213-226. In 1964, Shklovsky published a long and valuable critical biography of Tolstoy which he dedicated to Eikhenbaum.

85. Shklovsky never viewed the *skaz* as a primary and autonomous phenomenon, but it was a subject hotly debated throughout the twenties by some of the most important literary theoreticians of the time. *Skaz* is a prose narrative designed to exploit the peculiar point of view and speech of an unusual character. Eikhenbaum, is his already mentioned article on Gogol's "Overcoat" and in his article, "The Illusion of *Skaz*," viewed "oral speech" as the fundamental quality of the *skaz*. See "Illiuziia skaza," *Knizhnyi ugol*, 2 (1918), pp. 10-13; reprinted in *Skvoz' literaturu* (Leningrad, 1924).

86. This is *The Exploits of Brigadier Gerard*, published by Sir Arthur Conan Doyle in 1896. An old French soldier, veteran of the Napoleonic Wars, reminisces about his adventures. The stories are full of unexpected twists.

87. The reference is to Nikolai Semyonovich Leskov (1831-1895) and his famous short story "The Tale of the Left-handed Smith from Tula and the Steel Flea." Leskov is regarded as one of the most adept

practitioners of the *skaz*.

88. At this point, Shklovsky is expressing oblique criticism of Eikhenbaum's concept of the *dominanta*—the idea that a study of any author will reveal a basic principle that affects all his devices. Shklovsky objected to the idea that one device might control all the others, as he demonstrated in his attack on Potebnya, who ranked imagery as the supreme poetic device.

89. Vinogradov, Viktor Vladimirovich (1895-1969), a linguist and literary critic who became an eminent professor at Moscow University and a member of the Academy of Sciences. Shklovsky evidently feels that Vinogradov, like Potebnya and Eikhenbaum, has seized upon a secondary element of literary form and exaggerated its significance. In his studies of Akhmatova, for example, Vinogradov identified certain word clusters as the key to her work—a procedure which Eikhenbaurn criticized in his work on Akhmatova. See Victor Erlich, *Russian Formalism: History, Doctrine* (The Hague, 1955), pp. 202-203.

90. This is Hans Christian Andersen, whose fairy tale "The Old Street Lamp" serves as the basis for this portion of *Third Factory*. In Andersen's tale, the lamp is given, as a farewell gift, the power to remember all that it has seen and to show these visions to others. The latter is possible, however, only if it is supplied with a wax taper. The old couple who own it are unaware of its special powers and use it only for the mundane purpose of lighting their room. In the plight of the lamp, Shklovsky clearly sees parallels to his own predicament.

91. Yakubinsky, Lev Petrovich (d. 1946), a prominent Formalist critic and linguist. He joined the Party in the early twenties.

92. The aphorism means, "The spiritual does not comprehend the emotional." "*Miatel'* " is the archaic doublet of the set, which means "blizzard."

93. Marr, Nikolai Yakovlevich (1864-1934), a specialist in the Caucasian languages, especially Old Armenian and Old Georgian. His advocacy of the so-called Japhetic theory, which attempted to associate Basque, Etruscan and sometimes Sumerian and Elamite with the Caucasian languages, won the endorsement of Stalin and permitted him to become virtual dictator over Soviet linguistics during the early thirties.

94. An ancient Russian coin worth three kopeks.

95. A reference to *Seminary Sketches*, written by Nikolai Gerasimovich Pomyalovsky (1835-1863).

96. AUTHOR'S NOTE: Miklukha-Maklai [Nikolai Nikolaevich (1846-1888). An anthropologist and explorer of New Guinea, the

Papuans and the Western and Northern Micronesians. He organized an unsuccessful "free colony" on the coast of New Guinea and attempted to help the natives resist the British colonists.]

97. AUTHOR'S NOTE: Memoirs of Shenshin [Afanasy Afanasievich Fet (1820-1892).]

98. Elements of this story are based on fact. Petrograd actually had an antique shop called The Cheerful Native. It was located on Kronverk Prospekt (now Gorky Street) and was owned by I. N. Rakitsky, the mysterious man who lived in Gorky's household until Gorky's death in 1936. Rakitsky's nickname was Nightingale. His room, like the one in the story, was decorated with a pair of elephants, pictures of the tropics and a large divan covered with a frayed deerskin coat, which was the only source of heat in the room. See Shklovsky's book *O Maiakovskom*, (Moscow, 1940), pp. 115-116.

99. Jack the Witless is probably modeled on the Symbolist poet Vladimir Pyast, known for his eccentricity and his ubiquitous checked pants.

100. AUTHOR'S NOTE: Miklukha-Maklai.

101. Member of a religious sect which arose in the eighteenth century. Castration was often practiced as a means of insuring sexual abstinence.

102. AUTHOR'S NOTE: This may have actually happened to Captain Cook's ship.

103. Platonov, Andrei Platonovich (1899-1951), a writer who became famous posthumously when his unusual prose was rediscovered during the Thaw.

104. This is evidently the pump known as the Archimedes' Screw.

105. Rozanov, Vasily Vasilevich (1856-1919), Russian philospher, critic, and prose stylist of great influence.

106. Shub, Esfir Ilinichna (1894-1959), highly regarded editor and director of documentary films.

107. *Aeneid 3.70.* This line suggests a parallel between fallen Troy and fallen Petersburg, a parallel also used by Shklovsky in *Zoo, or Letters Not About Love*. The survivors of shattered Troy, leaving the dead and dying of the city behind them, set forth with the hope of preserving their culture in another land. They consider founding their city on a plain tilled by the Thracians, but as Aeneas uproots saplings to build an altar, blood oozes from the broken roots and the tormented spirit of Polydorus, a Trojan treacherously slain by the Thracian king, urges the refugees to leave this tainted soil. The line which ends *Third Factory* marks the departure of the Trojans for unknown and perilous shores.

Afterword

Every work of literature has a structure, and that structure consists entirely of the relations between the work's parts. This is one of Viktor Shklovsky's central tenets, and from it the many works of his long and productive life unfold. The interactive processes producing literary works—the motifs and motives, the movements and devices—are dynamic forces, intricate and complex linkages. They are workings, and hence, in the title of this book, the analogy to a factory.

But, even as it is generating a work of literature, Shklovsky's *Third Factory* is also at work on a larger production. His first factory, Shklovsky says near the beginning of the book, was "family and school. The second was *Opoyaz*. And the third—is processing me at this very moment." The "me" in question is not Viktor Shklovsky but "Viktor Shklovsky," a literary figure, one part among the many generating the never-complete sequence of writings that is ceaselessly creating and recreating the life of literature. This life has its structures too, and they too consist entirely of relations.

"A work of art," Shklovsky notes, "is perceived against a background of and by association with other works of art. The form of a work of art is determined by its relationship with other pre-existing forms. . . . All works of art, and not only parodies, are created either as a parallel or an antithesis to some model."[1]

The accuracy of this observation is amply demonstrated in Barrett Watten's "Correlation of 'Position' with *War and Peace*,"[2] a work Watten composed by inserting between the lines, taken in order, of his own poem, "Position," with paragraphs, picked from Tolstoy's novel blindly, as it were (the choice of paragraph was determined by use of a table of random numbers that sent Watten to the top of specific pages). What unfolds as the work progresses is an astonishing series of cross-interpretations, a cascade of illuminations, casting both works into the history of the other while creating a new work in the context of an ever-expanding literary world.

The work opens as follows:

The monument speaks correctly.

"Good day, General!" said he. "I have received the letter you brought from the Emperor Alexander and am very glad to see you." He glanced with his large eyes into Balashev's face and immediately looked past him.

To get results
that all might disappear.

"A town captured by the enemy is like a maid who has lost her honor," thought he (he had said so to Tuchkov at Smolensk). From that point of view he gazed at the Oriental beauty he had not seen before. It seemed strange to him that his long-felt wish, which had seemed unattainable, had at last been realized. In the clear morning light he gazed now at the city and now at the plan, considering its details, and the assurance of possessing it agitated and awed him.

As

extreme.

Viktor Shklovsky's monumental study of Tolstoy (*Lev Tolstoy*) was translated into English and published in Moscow by Progress Publishers in 1978. Watten had probably read that work by 1981, the year he composed "Correlation of 'Position' with *War and Peace*," and he was definitely familiar with Shklovsky's seminal essay, "Art as Technique" (also called "Art as Device"), which was included in Lee T. Lemon and Marion J. Reis's *Russian Formalist Criticism: Four Essays* of 1965; it is in this essay that Shklovsky offers his most fully elaborated discussion of the device he called *ostranenie* ("enstrangement"), using examples from Tolstoy, including two separate extended

100

passages from *War and Peace*, to demonstrate its function. It is evident that "Correlation of 'Position' with *War and Peace*," while being engaged explicitly with the works of Tolstoy, is addressed, at least implicitly, to Shklovsky as well.

And, I believe, Watten's 1979 trilogy *Plasma/Paralleles/"X"*[3] can be read similarly as an homage to Shklovsky.

The story of how the writings of the radical philologists, writers, and critics known as the Russian Formalists influenced (and at crucial points enlivened) the writings of the American avant-garde poets known as the Language writers remains largely untold. The Russian group developed in the context of the Russian Revolution. *Opoyaz* was formed in 1914 by a group of students at the University of St. Petersburg, in an environment of dusty buildings and windswept paths on Vasily Island across the Neva from the center of the city at the end of what came to be called Philological Street. Frustrated by the academic conservatism of the university and responsive to the revolutionary intellectual radicalism of the period, Viktor Shklovsky (along with Boris Eikhenbaum, L. P. Yakubinsky, Osip Brik, B. Kushner, E. D. Polivanov, and Yury Tynyanov) gathered to rethink the question of poetic language (*Opoyaz* is an acronym for *Obshchestvo isucheniya poeticheskogo yazyka*, or "The Society for the Study of Poetic Language").

The American movement developed in the context of the Vietnam War. Language writing emerged in the mid 1970s, principally in the San Francisco Bay Area and New York although important work was being done in Washington, DC, and a few other locations, in the milieu of the antiwar movement and wide ranging calls for social justice. Frustrated (and even enraged) by pervasive political hypocrisy and the atrocities resulting from racism, sexism, classism, and (ultimately) capitalism, the Language writers, both collectively and individually, and with results that differ greatly from author to author and work to work, undertook to rethink the structures of language and thereby expose and, hopefully, alter the world

101

views embodied in them.

Viktor Shklovsky's *Third Factory* was first published in 1926 in the USSR; it became available in English in 1977, when Richard Sheldon's subtle and beautiful translation of the work was published by Ardis. It was not the first of Shklovsky's books to appear in English, however. Sheldon's translation of *A Sentimental Journey* had appeared in 1970 (Cornell University Press) and his translation of *Zoo, or Letters Not About Love* came out the next year (Cornell University Press, 1971; reprinted by Dalkey Archive Press, 2001).

Lily Feiler's translation of Shklovsky's *Mayakovsky and His Circle* was published the year after that (Dodd, Mead, 1972).

Within a very few years, the writings of Viktor Shklovsky were being circulated among writers of the then emerging literary movement that has come to be known as Language writing. With the publication of the fourth edition of Victor Erlich's *Russian Formalism: History, Doctrine* in 1980 our interest in Russian Formalist work expanded and intensified. That same year, Kit Robinson's chapbook length collection, *Tribute to Nervous*, included two poems, "Zoo" and "Not About," whose titles come explicitly from Shklovsky's *Zoo, or Letters Not About Love*, phrases from which appear scattered through the poems.[4] "Plotless Literature," a chapter of Shklovsky's *Theory of Prose*, stood as the first essay in the first issue of *Poetics Journal* (January, 1982), initiating (and, in some sense, initialing) the publication in which many of the central essays of the Language writing movement first appeared.

Even before this, on March 18, 1979, Barrett Watten presented a talk on "Russian Formalism & The Present" (reprinted in *Total Syntax*, Southern Illinois University Press, 1985). During the discussion following the talk (some of which is included in the published version), Watten quotes a passage ("About a Red Elephant") from *Third Factory* and situates it as one of the models for his own poem, "Plasma," from which he also quotes:

They lost their sense of proportion. Nothing is the right size.

He walks in the door and sits down.

The road turns into a beautiful country drive. The voice isn't saying something, but turning into things.

Irregular movements spread out the matter at hand.

My work then is done.

His earliest dreams were prerecorded. Pointing a finger at a child in the act of play.

Light grows from the corners of the state map.

The universe is shaped like a hat. I lose interest and fall off the bed.

What the Shklovsky and Watten passages have in common are devices that were coming under examination in the works of a number of the Language writers during the late 1970s and early 1980s and that remain important elements in their work even now. We see narrative structures that are built through parallelism rather than consequence. The works feature paratactic arrays of "events" rather than a plot, so that "what will happen next" does indeed happen next, and next after that, and next again. Meanings (and the powerful emotionality that renders meaning meaningful) emerge cumulatively, unpredictably, and over time, as possibility, play, and position. Numerous and often non-linear logics are in force. As one sentence follows another, the reader expects a third to reveal an outcome, in the way that the final proposition of a syllogism resolves and concludes what the previous sentences began. But outcomes are deferred, and if they come at all they are unexpected. Enormous semantic pressure is exerted upon the connections between the sentences and a similarly strong syntactic pressure is exerted on the parts of any given sentence. The result is what Ron Silliman termed "the new sentence,"[5] a sentence that exhibits the pressure it is under by demonstrating torque, plasticity, and sometimes rupture. Examples abound in the works of the Language writers:

"Words from mouth now to talk in" (Ron Silliman, *Tjanting*).

"There are memories, but I am not that person" (Bob Perelman, *a.k.a*).

"such a thing should happen at all" (Bob Grenier, *Sentences*).

"Under the skin, / it's as if a woman / is fastening / five more flashlights / to the handlebars / of her bicycle" (Rae Armantrout, "Whole").

"A right angle wheels around the room, says 'nice arms' falling flat insistently, language doesn't want to do that" (Steve Benson, *Blue Book*).

"That too was a saturated structure, a day with adhesive sky" (Lyn Hejinian, *My Life*).

"I believe I made up the future in order to go away, to move elegantly" (Carla Harryman, *Under the Bridge*).

Along with the "new sentence," what I would term the "new paragraph" was also under construction in the late 1970s and early 80s, especially in the work of Carla Harryman, but also in Bob Perelman's *a.k.a.*, Kit Robinson's "Anamerican Paragraphs" and "A Sentimental Journey" (in his 1984 book, *Windows*), and Barrett Watten's *Plasma / Paralleles / "X"*. And if the "new sentence" owes something to Viktor Shklovsky, the "new paragraph" is clearly derived from his writing. The organizing principles of Shklovsky's prose (knots, loops, and bows, motifs that Shklovsky discusses in a long essay on the prose of Laurence Sterne[6]) emphasize the interrelatedness and equivalent status of an amazingly disparate array of things and events while simultaneously underscoring how crucially different from each other they are.

"I want to write about things and thoughts," he says in the opening chapter of *Third Factory*. What links the particular things and thoughts to each other is what Laurence Sterne's century knew as "sensibility" or "sentiment": a capacity for vivid affinity, empathy, friendship, art—and for irony. "There is much irony in a poet's beliefs," as Shklovsky points out. "They are, after all, full of mischief."[7]

In their heterogeneity, their subversive undercurrents, their way of achieving inclusion through use of digression while simultaneously using digressions as a means of being pointed, the works of Viktor Shklovsky are so appropriate to our contemporary situation as to seem to have been written for us. His writings do precisely what he has said it is art's goal to do: they "restore . . . sensation of the world," they "resurrect things and kill pessimism."[8]

Sensation of the world and a counter to pessimism are what the Language writers, when first encountering Shklovsky in the 1970s, found in his work. It is what remains for new readers to discover in the mischievous skepticism and driving hopefulness of *Third Factory*.

LYN HEJINIAN
2002

NOTES

1. Viktor Shklovsky, *Theory of Prose*, tr. Benjamin Sher (Dalkey Archive Press, 1990), 20.

2. A portion of the work appears in *Aerial* 8, an issue of the magazine devoted to Watten's work (*Aerial* 8, 1995).

3. Originally published by Tuumba Press; reprinted in Barrett Watten, *Frame (1971-1990)* (Sun & Moon Press, 1997).

4. Kit Robinson, *Tribute to Nervous* (Tuumba Press, 1980).

5. Ron Silliman, "The New Sentence," first presented as a talk in 1977 and published in Ron Silliman, *The New Sentence* (Roof Books, 1987).

6. Viktor Shklovsky, "The Novel as Parody: Sterne's *Tristram Shandy*," in *Theory of Prose*, 147-170.

7. *Theory of Prose*, 185.

8. Viktor Shklovsky, "Resurrection of the Word," tr. Richard Sherwood, in *Russian Formalism: A Collection of Articles and Texts in Translation*, ed. Stephen Bann and John E. Bowlt (Scottish Academic Press, 1973), 46.

SELECTED DALKEY ARCHIVE PAPERBACKS

FOR A FULL LIST OF PUBLICATIONS, VISIT:
www.dalkeyarchive.com